Peter Legaard Nielsen, born in 1960, is a Danish author, who made his debut with a poetry collection, *The Bloody Temple of the Heart*, in 1985 and had his breakthrough with the novel, *While the Sun Slowly Burns Up*, in 1987. *Darkness Without Limits* is his second novel. He has published 9 novels and 2 poetry collections and edited a large number of anthologies.

He was chairman of the Danish Fiction Writers Association from 1997–2001 and from 2002–2007. In 1992, he was awarded a 3-year grant from the state's Art Fund. He was a literary reviewer at a newspaper from 1987 to 1992.

Peter is also an Authorized Advanced Rolfer™ and an Authorized Level 3 IFS Practitioner.

Peter Legaard Nielsen

DARKNESS WITHOUT LIMITS

Translated by Ole Thienhaus

AUSTIN MACAULEY PUBLISHERS™

LONDON • CAMBRIDGE • NEW YORK • SHARJAH

Ordering Information
Quantity sales: Special discounts are available on quantity purchases by corporations, associations, and others. For details, contact the publisher at the address below.

Publisher's Cataloging-in-Publication data
Nielsen, Peter Legaard
Darkness Without Limits

ISBN 9781647504366 (Paperback)
ISBN 9781647508777 (ePub e-book)

Library of Congress Control Number: 2024905208

www.austinmacauley.com/us

First Published 2024
Austin Macauley Publishers LLC
40 Wall Street, 33rd Floor, Suite 3302
New York, NY 10005
USA

mail-usa@austinmacauley.com
+1 (646) 5125767

20240625

Part 1

The noise is loud and insistent. Half-asleep, I reach out my hand and fumble for the alarm clock, but it is not where it usually is. So, I draw my blanket over my ears instead, and when the annoying ringing stops, I fall asleep again. The next thing I notice is that there is a pull on my arm. With difficulty, I open my sleep-heavy eyes and see that Mom is standing there, leaning down over my bed. Her face, which is long and narrow with a round forehead, is glowing in the light that streams down from the ceiling lamp. In one hand, she has a yellow comb that she is dragging through her black, permed hair with small, impatient jerks, while she continues to pull on me with the other.

"It's almost seven o'clock. You fell asleep with the light on," she says and leans forward and swings the lamp over my head. "What time was it when you went to sleep? Two? Three?"

"Four," I mumble.

"Let's hope that's not true."

I don't have a clue how much time has passed when I sense, through my sleep, that she is standing again by my bedside.

"Have you still not gotten up?"

An open book slides heavily over the side of the bed and lands noisily on the floor as I rise on my elbows and look at her with pinched eyes.

"This is really stupid," she says. "Now you've read the whole night long again."

She picks up the book and puts it on the table where the alarm clock sits at the wrong end. It shows that it is quarter past seven.

"It ends up that you turn nights into days, if you keep going this way," she says.

I mumble some incomprehensible words and slide back into sleep and into the pulsating warmth under the blanket. Next, the blanket is being ripped off, and I curl up in the cold air and cross my arms.

"Won't you please let me stay put?" I say.

I have a disturbing premonition that this is one of the gray days, barely worth calling days, when it will be impossible for me to be awake even if I stand up. One of the days when I know that the only thing I feel like doing is to hide in my room behind a locked door. And no change occurs during the night while I sleep.

"It's really up to you," she says. "I don't want to go through this trouble with you every morning. From now on, you can decide for yourself when you get up."

There is the sound of a slight creak as her steps disappear toward the door opening, and I raise myself up in surprise and look around in the empty room. I didn't think that she really meant that. She is not one to give up. Although I know that I shouldn't, I reach down over the side of the bed and pull the blanket that lies in a heap on the floor over myself.

I fall asleep and begin to dream uneasily. I am in a dark underground toilet where the water runs down over the white tiles and out over the rim onto a full sink. I am sitting, in fear, on a chair in the middle of the cold room while the water is rising up around my feet. In my hands, I have two photographs.

"Confess," says a deep angry man's voice.

There is a sharp white light that blinds me so that it is only with difficulty and through pinched eyes that I can see the two photos, from which Mom and Dad are smiling up at me.

"Confess," shouts the voice. "Confess."

But I don't know what it is that I have done, and I lower my head, worried.

Now I notice that someone is breathing onto the back of my neck, and while I am turning around, my heart starts pounding hard. In front of me stands my old English teacher. From his nostrils and out of his ear, small black hairs stick out, and his eyes are staring at me.

"Look at the scars," he says.

His fleshy lips form the words. They come out slowly and clearly with emphasis on each letter.

"Take a look at the scars. The scars of imagination."[1]

---

[1] Italics indicate that original is in English.

Something cold and wet, a stream of water, hits me in the face, and I get up, shocked, and blink my eyes. At first, I don't understand what happened. I realize that my face is still wet and catch sight of Mom who stands at the bottom of my bed with an empty glass in her hands and smiles, triumphant and scared.

"Did…did you throw water on me?" I stammer. "What…what kind of bullshit is that!"

"Well, you've come awake," she says and laughs nervously. "Can you get up now?"

I'm mad as I lift my legs out over the side of the bed, and I grow even more incensed when I notice how the cold drops are running down over my face and seeping through my pajama jacket. I take the book Mom put on the table and place it on the bookshelf along the far wall. Then I walk toward the window, yawn discreetly, and stretch.

It is a cold morning with clear stars in the sky. From the bathroom window where the ice flowers grow along the edges of the glass, I can see the dark, leafless branches of the trees that stand in front of the long row of glowing streetlights and, farther away, the hunch-backed house roofs with their thick layer of freshly fallen snow. The snow that covers the lawn shines in a supernatural white in the pale moonlight, and it seems as if the garden were full of shadows. I turn around to the mirror and pull off, half crazed, my wet pajama jacket while I am looking at my face with hostility. I'm tired, having slept little and poorly. I notice how a familiar, frightening and ridiculous feeling of being responsible for everything is coming up inside me. I can't get used to having no one to talk to. I am feeling incredibly tired, and it is as though there is nothing worth getting up for. I lean forward and run my hand over the scattered beard bristles on my chin.

"Well, get a grip now," I tell myself at the thought of yet another indifferent day.

I rise up and step in under the shower.

While I am looking for the faucets, Mom calls from the kitchen, "Remember to clean up after yourself."

Through the wall, I can hear her talk to herself. Her voice sounds angry, and though I try to avoid it, I become annoyed. I don't know what it could be, but it sounds as if I have done something wrong. I bend down and carefully dry the tiles.

A bit later, I step out into the kitchen where it is so warm that the windowpane is gray with condensation. I sit down at the table and start eating the food Mom has put in front of me. Meanwhile, she goes back and forth, slamming drawers and cupboard doors. This morning she is wearing a white blouse with a long bow at the neck and black, freshly ironed slacks. She has applied a discrete blue eyeshadow, some skin powder and a bit of lipstick. I am looking at her out of the corner of my eyes until she leaves the kitchen. A little later, she comes back.

"You forgot to turn off the faucets," she says.

"Impossible."

"Don't you believe I have eyes in my head?"

She walks to the stove and removes the old, grease-spotted newspapers covering the burners that have not been in use since last night. She is still talking to herself, while she is crumpling up the papers and throwing them in the trashcan. Her voice sounds threatening. I turn my face away and start reading the text on a milk carton but without grasping what it says. A feeling grabs hold of me, half hopelessness, half panic.

"You are falling asleep sitting there. Wake up," says Mom.

She is standing in the doorway, with my coat over her arm. I don't know why I'm doing it, only that I can't stop myself, as I slowly and without saying a word reach out for the milk carton and fill my glass. She bites her lip.

"It's not going to be long till you have to go. Tell me, do you do this deliberately?"

She is standing in the doorway and waiting for me to answer, and, when I don't, she turns around and hangs my coat back on the clothes rack. She sits down in front of me and hides her face in her hands. I am almost certain of what she will say, and for the first time I am nervously looking up at the clock on the wall. If I want to be on time, I should be going now.

"Are you aware," she says and looks up, "that you behave more and more strangely? You lie on your bed in your room all afternoon and all evening—until you go to bed. You are always in that room. What do you do? Stare at the wallpaper?"

"Will you please leave me in peace," I say angrily and take hold of the glass. "I can't understand why it's just me that you talk to this way. With other people, you're always so friendly."

She cradles her face in her hands and draws a deep breath.

10

"How can it be that you never see other people? You never step outside your door. Is there anything at all that interests you? I thought that at least you'd like to pass your exam. You've got to pull yourself together."

I drink a swallow of milk and set the glass back on the table, hard.

Mom tries to catch my eyes.

"I have talked to Dad about this," she says and lowers her voice. "It kind of reminds me of the last time. Do you remember that? Is this a repeat of that, is that what you want?"

I have reached the point that, if she says one more thing, I'll be jumping up.

"Wow, it's about time I get out of here."

My skin is stinging, and I am trying hard to pretend that I have not heard what she said.

Mom leans back and looks up at me in surprise.

"Take it easy. I've set all clocks a half-hour ahead to make sure you get out of here in time."

"You did what...?" I say weakly and drop back, against my will, down on my seat. "No, I'm going now," I say and jump up again.

While I'm buttoning up my coat, Mom comes into the hallway.

"What time is it for real?" I ask when it looks as though she wants to continue our conversation.

I'm setting my watch.

"Are you sure I can make it?"

"Yes, there's time enough."

She is leaning against the doorframe.

"What's wrong with you?" she asks.

"There's nothing wrong with me," I say.

The sky has begun to lighten up as I step out onto the stairs. There is a sharp cold wind that blows the snow into my face, and I bow my head and put up the collar of my coat while I'm walking down to the sidewalk. After a long while, I catch sight of the bus stop and the yellow sign that sticks out vertically from a snowdrift.

* * *

The conversation with Mom keeps ringing in my ears with an alarming insistence. "...about to remind me of last time..."

"...a repeat of that, is that what you want?"

"...is that what you want?" I take my books and pen case out of my bag, and while I'm waiting for the bell to ring in the first period, I find the time to look around. The walls are a weak light blue, and the windows sit up so high that barely a piece of colorless sky is visible. Behind the teacher's desk, on the wall farthest away, hangs a blackboard with white traces of chalk.

I can hear that the girls and boys I go to classes with have begun to talk and laugh out in the hallway. Shortly after, when the bell rings, they come in through the door in small groups. I put my chin on my arms and yawn sleepily while they proceed to their seats. Although we are in the same class, I don't know any of them really well. It's been many years since I needed to make a big detour to come home from school because the guys in my class were waiting for me every day to give me a beating, but I still have a sense that it's safest not to attract any attention. I have, nearly all the time, a sense of not belonging.

Andersen walks in and closes the door behind him. He puts his briefcase on the desk, takes his glasses off and cleans them on his shirtsleeve. Then he turns toward us as if he just now realized that we are here, and he says, "Good morning."

I sit up and see that Vibeke who sits at the first table leans forward and whispers into the ear of her friend Helle who laughs. At the next table sits Lars with his chair angled back against the wall. For a moment, I'm looking at his brown, short-clipped hair and his straight nose which continues on to his forehead. Thus, I let my sight move on along the row and look uneasily out through the window.

I'm aware that the others don't like me, and that they even try to avoid me, but I don't understand at all why. Do I act wrong, or do I say the wrong things? Was I too anxious to make a good impression at the beginning? I try to think about the expectations I have had since two and a half years ago. At that time, I simply imagined that high school would be a new start. In any case, I had not anticipated that I would be even more lonely than I was before. I think that, all the time, I'm trying to work on myself to be like them.

Some days, when we sit in class, or when I listen to the others during recess, I get a strange, disturbing feeling that I am quite slowly disappearing in their silence and aloofness. I look under the tabletop, and for a moment I have such a strong feeling of hatred toward this place and these people that I'm scared. I wish I knew why other people think that there is something wrong with me.

Andersen has gone to the blackboard which he fills with rows of irregular verbs. I lean back and look down at my hands. Even though I've tried all morning to avoid it, the mystifying dream of the photos keeps showing up in my thoughts. I clench my fists, then stretch out my fingers, and watch how the sinews move under the skin.

I hadn't noticed anything when suddenly a shadow leans in over my seat. I lift up my head in confusion and see that Andersen is standing in front of me, and that several of the others have a hand up in the air. Now I realize that I'm sitting in an embarrassing, awkward position, and I raise myself up. I hope no one has noticed.

"Yes, that was you who I asked. What do you say?" asks Andersen and bangs a wrist down on my desk.

"What?" I mumble, and my cheeks turn red.

From several tables around me, there is the sound of gleeful giggles.

"Will you kindly repeat the question?" I say.

* * *

It's almost dark, and I have turned on the light above the desk so that I can read the paper. The ad is small and seems odd, and it's pure coincidence that I spotted it. It is printed on one of the last pages after buy-and-sell classifieds and before the death notices. I experience a weak, indistinct excitement and read it once more to be sure I understand its meaning. It seems to speak to me directly. I sit back in my chair and read it a third time. Then I lean forward, find a pair of scissors in the desk drawer and cut it out.

The book I read while lying on my bed is dense with its many small letters and its never-ending procession of words that move across the page: It gives me a strange sense of excitement, nervousness and dizziness. It's not what I'm reading that gives me that sense, but the sight of the dark, blurred words and sentences covering page after page.

There is a knock on the door, and Mom calls that we must eat. I put the book down and go out to the kitchen where Dad is sitting, bent over, at the table. He has placed his forearms on each side of the plate, and the light falling down on him from the ceiling lamp makes the bald spot on his scalp shine. I pull out my chair and sit down across from him. Mom puts a pot on the table and takes her apron off. She folds it carefully and lays it in the drawer under the table. Dad is busy cutting into small pieces the meat with which he has had a hard time since he lost his teeth.

"What are you thinking about?" he asks and turns his face toward me while he is chewing.

"Nothing."

"Well, now," he says and swallows a piece of meat whole. "I thought it was your future that occupied you so much."

"What do you mean?"

"Well, you've almost finished the last year of high school. It's not all that strange if I'm asking what you imagine you'll be doing afterwards."

"I haven't thought about that."

Dad lowers his head. He sticks his fork into a new piece of meat and starts cutting it.

"Who cut something out of the paper?" Mom asks.

I'm looking up.

"That was me."

"What is it that you cut out?"

"Not much. That was just an ad. I trust there was nothing important on the other side?"

"No. I was just wondering that the paper was not in its usual place. You know well that it is supposed to be placed in the paper holder."

She directs her eyes to Dad's plate.

"Is the meat cooked well enough?"

He settles on mumbling an answer that could mean both yes and no.

We continue eating in silence, and when we're done, I go back to my room. I switch on the lamp and lie down on my bed and look up at the white ceiling. For a long time, my mind is completely blank. I take the ad from my pocket and slowly read it yet another time. Then I turn on my side and look out through the dark windowpane. I can hear Mom and Dad talking with each other in the kitchen. Shortly afterwards they go into the living room, and the television is turned on. I put the ad back in my pocket and stretch out my unwilling hand and pick up the book that lies open on the table.

"Watch out!" shouts Mom and grabs the handle on the inside of the car door. "Listen, it's always very slippery right here. I can still remember well the time the car went into a spin."

It's Sunday afternoon. The warm air blows full-steam, and the inside of the car smells heavy and sweet of the perfume Mom puts on when we go on a visit.

She turns around toward me.

"The car was simply spinning around. Within a blink of an eye, we ended up on the opposite lane and were on our way downhill again."

I can't help grinning.

"That's nothing to grin at," she says. "Imagine if there had been an oncoming car."

"Can you really remember that?" asks Dad without moving his sight from the roadway.

"Can I?" she shouts and turns her head forward again. "I had to walk on foot to the top of the hill because you just had to play the hero and tempt fate."

"Maybe it wasn't because of my poor driving that we didn't make it quite up the hill?" asks Dad.

His hairy hands rest calmly on the steering wheel, and I can see his blue eyes in the rearview mirror. Mom stretches out one hand along the stick shift and puts it on his thigh.

"Right," she says.

She raises her hand up to the back of his neck and strokes it down over the edge of his short gray hair. Her movements cause me to feel embarrassed, and I turn around and look out at the trafficked country roads that cut through the snow-covered fields like black strings. Far away are standing some skiers on a hill. At the sight of them, I become aware of a bit of jealousy. I think about how other young people make their Sunday fun. Surely not as boring as mine. But I don't know what else I should do.

I'm sitting up. We must be somewhere in proximity to where the exit is to the address named in the ad. I stick my hand in my pocket to make sure I still have it on me.

A little later Dad drives up to the curb.

"Here we are," he says.

Mom releases her tight grip on the door handle.

The living room is dark and warm with the dry air from the radiators. After shaking hands and saying hello, we sit down at the large dining table that sits in the middle of the floor beneath an old-fashioned crystal chandelier. Everywhere, along the walls and in the corners, there's furniture that causes the room to appear overstuffed and smaller than it is. It's become quiet, and it seems as though the stillness is timeless, like eternity, and like the loud ticking from the clock on the mantle is but a rhythm that underscores the timelessness. I'm sitting and thinking that a whole world will come to a standstill on the day when Grandma no longer has the strength in her gout-ridden hand to wind up the clock.

Small and hunched over, she walks in her sloppy slippers through the kitchen and the living room to get the coffee pot and some plates with cookies. From the well-worn easy chair where Grandpa is sitting there rises blue smoke from a cigar he smokes half-lost in thought.

"Judgment Day is coming soon," says Grandma and sits down.

She pushes a gray tuft of hair in under her hairnet with a vain, almost coy, movement. Her face has an expression of fake saintliness.

"What are you saying?" exclaims Mom and puts her cookie down on the plate.

"It's in the paper."

"I don't understand," says Mom sharply. "I haven't read that. Do you think you need stronger glasses?"

Grandma shakes her head slowly. She is leaning forward and pinching her eyes into two small dots.

"No, I always take my glasses off when I read the paper. There's more than enough eyesight left for me to make out the headlines. It's the same regardless of what you read. The world is about to end. The end time has arrived. I really don't care to know what will happen in detail."

She leans back in her chair and purses her mouth and looks searchingly for a shift in our eyes. Her hands are beginning to stroke down her apron.

"To him who understands and can see," she says, "the newspaper is full of prophecies. There's writing on the wall. The end time has come. The Evil One lays his eggs everywhere, but it is humans who hatch them. The spawn of Satan—"

"That's enough," says Mom, "I don't want to hear another word."

Grandma smiles and looks down at her hands that glide back and forth along the edge of her apron. I have a slight feeling of anxiety, reminding me how dark and threatening everything was. It's like I can't lift my eyes. From over in his easy chair, Grandpa, deeply settled in, sends a waft of smoke out into the room. None of us says a word.

In the corner between the two doors, there is a green pull-out sofa. I can remember that it has always been there, that I had to sleep on it when I came to visit. Grandma's bed sheets were blue and stiff, and a breath of cold air wafted over from them when she carried them up from the cupboard in the basement. One of my favorite things was to lie down between the bed sheets, and while my fingers struggled with the buttons of my clothes, I got them opened fast and jumped up onto the sofa. The cotton closed me in cold, and I could feel how a shudder ran up and down my spine and caused me goose pimples. Restless and wound up, I threw myself from side to side to find the least cold spots. I was in a state of unrestrained joy where only my body and the fabric were real. I was in a different world where there were no trolls. Right on the other side of the door, in the darkness under the stairs leading up to the ceiling, they were waiting.

The door out to the staircase stands open, and a sinister set of stairs comes toward me. I'm crawling on my knees from step to step and, scared, stop several times to look back and make sure the troll under the staircase is not following me. The door to the ceiling slides open with difficulty. Warm, stagnant air hits me and causes me to gasp for breath as I take my first steps over the floorboards into the semi-dark room. Under the roof, there are blocks sticking out in the weak light that comes in through cracks between the bricks and the little peephole in the gable. A bit farther away, a soft squeal sounds from the big wooden pipe which is drawn back and forth under the box with the two rocks giving it weight. Up above, sheets and blankets are hanging to dry, and in the chimney with its peeling paint, there is a singing as though there were a man inside it, playing the flute. I walk in among the sheets and know all of a sudden how I can go about taking Grandma by surprise. Surrounded by the bulging sheet of fabric I find my way to the darkest corner where she thinks no one is.

The pipe stops, and I hurry as quickly as I can into the dark. A sound of dragging steps is spreading out over the floor, and I already feel in my stomach how the laughter chuckles. For a long time, I stand quite still and listen for the faintest sign of a noise to reveal where Grandma is. The man in the chimney keeps playing the flute, and the bed sheets and blankets wave lightly. I take a step forward and see, right away, out of the corner of my eyes a shadow that moves, bent over, through the darkness. I stumble and grab hold of the nearest sheet which slides soundlessly to the floor and reveals something new behind it. On my short, unsteady legs I hasten toward the door, fighting with the large piece of fabric that seems to hang in my way on purpose. I'm caught in a labyrinth of sheets and blankets.

Feeling nothing but anguish, I curl myself up on the dusty floor and roll, kicking my legs, under the pieces of fabric. Immediately, fluttering, quick fingers grab hold of my ankles to drag me back into the dark. I let out a shriek and then lie quite still with terror. The long-armed creature that is lurking for me in the shadow, may, for all I know, not realize that I am lying just here. With a violent effort, I roll forward and come to stand on my legs and reach the door in short steps while the rustling of the sheets reveals that the beast is in pursuit. I beat my fists hard against the door, and I know that now, now, the troll will take me. It howls in the chimney, and it screams inside my body. Finally, I can no longer hold back the noise. I feel the burning grip of a cold hand around my arm, and I remember that Grandpa told us that he found the bones of a skeleton the first time he cleaned out the chimney.

"Mom," I shout and bang my fists against the door, but nobody hears me. I sink down on my knees and hide my face against the doorframe. "Dear God, I don't want to die."

With infinite slowness so as not to make any noise, I crawl over into the nearest corner. My heart is pounding, and I dare not look back. I sit down with my back toward the room and hide my face in my hands that lie on my knees.

"Don't let the troll find me. Dear God, call my mom."

Much later, when the light has changed its position, there is the sound of a cry and steps on the staircase.

"Where are you? Where are you?"

I stay put, unable to move and not daring to make a sound. The door opens, and steps come nearer. A hand takes hold of my arm and shakes it.

"What are you doing?" asks a voice that sounds like Mom's. "Why are you in hiding?"

My body is slowly being turned around and my hands taken away from my eyes. With the movement the stiffness disappears from my body, and in the dazzling light I look into a face that looks as if it were surrounded by gold. So, He has heard me after all. I begin to cry with relief that I am not going to die, and I fall onto her breast. The smooth fabric feels soft against my cheek, and I bury my face in it until I am completely out.

"Has anything else happened?" asks Mom and moves restlessly in her seat.

Grandma gets up and pours coffee into our cups. She sits down again, and it becomes quiet again, except for the clock that keeps ticking. I start tapping impatiently with my fingers on the chair leg.

"Well, I think it's about time we drive home," says Mom and looks over at Dad.

Outside it is already almost dark. Mom collects her coat and steps into the car.

"I can't understand," she says, "why Mom keeps on scaring me."

"Now, let's not discuss that again, ok?" says Dad and puts the key in the ignition.

"Understood. I guess I'll never get rid of that feeling."

* * *

Through the open door comes the sound of Mom's and Dad's voices into the living room, they are low and angry. It's been several hours since I've come home. And I'm lying on the bed reading.

"I should have listened to Dad and Mom. They advised me against getting married to a man twenty-three years older than me," says Mom.

"At the time, you had no objection."

"I left."

"Yes, but you came back."

I get up and close the door.

A bit later it opens. I turn around in surprise and see that Dad is coming in. He walks up to the window and stands silently, with his back against it. I put the book away, and I'm looking at his bent-over figure for a long time. Usually either he or Mom comes in to bother me. I hope he hasn't come to ask me to take his side as he usually does when they have had an argument.

"Did you want something?" I ask.

Dad turns around and looks me in the face for a brief moment.

"Yes," he says and sits down carefully in the chair at my desk.

"What are you doing?"

"I'm reading."

"It's odd that you never get tired of that," he says. "Don't you ever feel lonely? In any case, I was never alone that much when I was young."

"I'm not lonely," I say.

For a long time, nothing happens. Dad is sitting there without moving, in his light gray shirt, sleeves rolled up, and staring down at the floor between his black woolen pant legs. His wrinkled face is without any expression. I get up and sit across from him. He lifts a hand and strokes the back of his neck, then he is sitting quite still again.

"What is it you want?" I ask and pick up a pencil.

"Well," he says and clears his throat. "I have just had an argument with Mom. She is saying…"

"I don't want to hear it," I say.

He falls silent and looks hurt.

"There was also another reason I came," he says. "Mom has asked me to have a serious talk with you. I understand that she has a hard time getting you up for school in the morning. Don't you think that seems a bit ridiculous, considering how old you are? After all, you're eighteen."

"Yes," I say.

Dad looks at me expectantly, and I exclaim, "I don't know what it is…It's not just the people or this place. It reminds me of … You know…You know what I'm thinking of."

He is at first looking at me with confusion, then a worried expression comes into his eyes.

"I trust you haven't begun to get some of your weird ideas?" he asks and wrinkles his forehead.

"No, of course I haven't," I say and put the pencil that has started to tremble between my fingers, down on the table.

Dad leans back and puts his hands on his knees. He looks out the window and then redirects his light blue eyes on to me.

"It's strange," he says. "By and by, I come to wonder if I know you. It is as though it was just yesterday that you were a little fellow who clung to my hand…and today you've grown taller than me."

Again, he lets his gaze slide down to the floor between his legs.

"At the time, I did not think that you were anything but a detached part of myself…an amputated body part…yeah, that you were created from my rib. And now we are sitting here facing each other like two strangers."

Absentmindedly, I pick up the pencil again and start tilting it up and down uneasily. Dad and I have really always been strangers to each other—there's nothing new here. I can recall how I had to bend my neck over backward to look up his enormous body to his face that contrasted with the sky, his nose being a big triangle. Dad has always been distant, unapproachable, his face way up there, even after I grew taller than him. For some reason I don't grasp, I'm getting angry.

"I don't know," continues Dad, "when it dawned on me that you're quite different than I had imagined. You were afraid of almost everything. I can remember how you came running to me each time a jet flew over the house. You would stand there with your head between my legs and press your ears against my knees. You've got to understand that we had to give you a sturdy upbringing."

"That upbringing," I say, "has taken its toll. Or left its marks is maybe a better way of putting it."

I'm staring down at the tabletop, and I can see the hated brown belt, meant for me, that I first had to pull out from between the straps in his pants. But what I remember best is the unreal feeling when I would stand in front of him, my pants down, and didn't know what I was being punished for. One day he held his hands out for me to hand him the belt, and I struck him as hard as I could on the back of his hand. I had not meant to do that. It was as if it happened of its own accord. I can remember that I was waiting for him to beat me yet harder than usual. Instead, he let out a shriek of fright and pain and got tears in his eyes. He simply turned around and left. For a long time afterwards, I was afraid that the punishment would come when I least expected it, but he never again tried to beat me.

Dad has bowed his head and is looking down at his hands which he opens and closes several times.

"It's only the hard steel that rings out," he says and sounds as though it were he himself whom he is trying to convince.

He leans forward and it looks as though he is about to stand up. Then he leans back again.

"There's something else I've thought about and want to talk to you about," he says and tries to look me in the eyes, "let's say 'man to man'."

I turn my face and look out the window. Perhaps it's the tone of his voice that gives me a creepy foreboding of what he is going to say. In truth, I'd just like to slap my hands over my ears so as not to hear another word. It's just always Dad who has the last word. It's just always Dad who has said what's right and wrong without explaining why. I can barely stand the thought that he is an ordinary human being.

He lets his shoulders slide forward and sinks down in his chair.

"I believe that we have always endeavored to show you how a person should behave. There is so much around us that is inhumane, so much evil. Everything we usually don't talk about. I have learned that one must know one's place and always stand by one's name: That way, one can never go wrong."

"Have I done something wrong?" I ask in surprise.

"No, but we can't constantly keep an eye on what you're up to. We are worried about what's becoming of you...you know...it reflects back on us too."

"Damn it," I say. "I spend most of my time in here, in my room."

"Yes, but there are so many traps. Women are not always what they pretend to be."

I'm beginning to sweat. It's obvious that Dad finds it hard to utter the words. He opens and closes his mouth several times without saying anything. Until the words come out in a jerky way:

"We've never talked about these kinds of things. There are women..."

He pauses and looks, again, down at his hands.

"I think you must watch out. You have reached the age when..."

I quickly look up at him, so embarrassed that I'm close to curling my toes.

"Dad, all that I've known for years," I say.

I can't quite make myself tell him that his concerns are pretty ridiculous. I'm sure that if I were to get a girl to follow me down the street, I'd have to twist my arm around her.

He looks down, and his face twitches.

"I just meant that I had to say that."

I put the pencil back on the table and smile cautiously.

"You don't need to say more."

Dad's face is slowly lighting up. He gets a grip of the chair with both hands and stands up.

"Good. I think that the two of us understand each other. And maybe I can also tell Mom that as of today she will no longer have any trouble with you?"

"Yes," I say heavily.

He walks toward the door, and some of my tension goes away. Then he turns again, just as he is about to take hold of the doorknob.

"You know that you can always come to me if there's something you want to talk about."

"Yes," I say.

He closes the door behind him. I remain on my chair. I am certain that I will never ever come to ask him about anything.

* * *

The light from the overhead lamp in the car is so weak that I have to pinch my eyes to decipher the address at the bottom of the ad. Since I cut it out, I have taken it out and read it many times, and it still gives me the same unclear feeling of excitement and tension. It seems like I've driven too far. I turn off the lights and look out through the darkness for a light among the tree trunks. The first stretch of the way was the same one we usually drive when we have to visit Grandma and Grandpa, but the last section, through the woods, I don't know very well. I cast a look back over my shoulder, shift gears and turn the car onto the narrow road. My hands tremble slightly on the steering wheel with anticipation and nervousness.

The snow that lies along the roadside is shining in the weak light from the moon above the treetops. In the cone of light from the headlights, I fix my eyes on the driveway to a narrow gravel road that is almost hidden by the tall fir trees. That must be the reason I had not noticed it until then. I turn into the driveway and can hear the hanging tree branches scrape against the roof. After I have driven a few kilometers, the forest disappears, and a flat terrain with low growth vegetation opens up on both sides. I must be on the way down to the sea.

Ever since I drove out of the city, the darkness has filled me with a comfortable sensation of being alone. I look out through the windshield on to the desolate, harsh landscape where, in many places, the snow has been blown out over the middle of the roadway, and I come to think about what I'll do if the car gets stuck. Fortunately, there are fresh tire marks in the snow which show that recently other cars have driven here. They may be headed for the same place as me.

Still, no house appears, and even though the tire marks continue, I'm beginning to get the feeling that I have driven the wrong way. After having driven yet a few more kilometers while the road goes downhill toward the sea, I pull over and stop on the side of the road. I turn on the light and take the ad out of my pocket. As far as I can tell, this is the right way. I lean forward and continue slowly while scanning things through the windshield. I'm about to turn around as the road is turning desolate. It may be just coincidence that the other cars drove here. At that moment, I catch sight of a weak light coming from a row of windows.

At the end of the gravel road sits a farm in the shadow under a high, steep slope. I drive in among ten to twelve cars in the courtyard and turn off the engine. The farm has three buildings and is painted white, and there is light in all the windows in the main building. In the corner by the stable grow three small, wind-swept trees.

I step out into the snow, and I notice the cold air has a sharp salty odor. I can hear the sea a little way off. The thought of having to meet strangers makes me nervous while I'm walking up to the farmhouse. I make sure that the house number above the front door is correct and grab the door handle. After a moment of having felt the cold metal against my palm, I let go and drop my hand. I can still turn around. But then I force myself to press the door handle down, and I step into a small dark entry hall with two doors. Behind one of them I can hear a low murmur of voices. I knock.

"Come in," says a slightly hoarse woman's voice.

I open the door and stop still, embarrassed. On the floor in front of me, there stands a woman surrounded by a semicircle of people who are sitting on the ground. Everyone has turned their faces toward me. The room has a low ceiling, white walls, and is only weakly illuminated. It is nearly empty, and the curtains are drawn closed. The only one to stand out is the woman.

I stand there in surprise and take in things in the room and the people on the floor, but first and foremost I get an overwhelming impression of the woman. I don't know why but she seems extraordinary, like one of those people you take note of in any get-together.

"Come on in," she says and smiles. "You can hang your jacket up on the coat stand over there in the corner."

I hang up my coat and sit down on the outside of the row of people. There is an expectant silence in the room. I glance around from face to face at the people who are sitting there, and a couple of times I lock eyes. I don't know what I had expected, but in any case, they look like they're completely ordinary people. Again, I turn my eyes toward the woman.

She has slightly slanted eyes and high cheekbones, and her skin is very pale. Her hair, which is rich, curly, and black with gray stripes, hangs down over her shoulders and back. She is wearing a red shiny dress that sits tight on her well-toned and muscular body and emphasizes her chest and narrow hips. She is not particularly tall and built slight, but nonetheless I get the sense that she fills the entire room with her presence. It is as if she is different from the people I know. Then it occurs to me: She appears unusually alive.

The door is being closed, and a man and a woman with flushed faces enter. The woman says hello, and they quickly get out of their overcoats and settle down at the far end of the circle.

The woman is smiling and lets her gaze slide over our faces.

"Shouldn't we get started?" she says in a soft, slightly nasal voice. "I don't know if anyone else is coming. My name is Louise." She kneels down on the floor and pulls her legs up under herself. "As we are getting underway, I would like to offer a couple of explanations on a few things that may not have been obvious from the ad. Don't worry, I won't carry on with a long philosophical exposition or with mysterious generalizations. But I know that some folks feel uneasy with what I stand for. I want us all to be in the clear."

She looks around at us with a smile. Then she lays her hands on her knees and leans forward. "It's very simple and not a bit mysterious," she says. "It's all about saying one hundred percent 'yes' to life."

The house is dark when I come back two hours later. I didn't tell anybody I was leaving, and, so as not to wake up Mom and Dad, I stick the key carefully into the lock and tiptoe through the hallway. I open the door to the living room and fumble for the light switch, but just as I manage to press it, the floor lamp comes on. I blink my eyes in surprise and look at Mom who is sitting in an easy chair in her red kimono, legs tucked up underneath her.

"Aren't you guys asleep?"

She gathers the kimono around her and puts her feet into her slippers.

"Where have you been?"

"I have to get up early," I say. "I'm going right to bed."

"One moment," she says. "There's something here that doesn't add up. You've been sitting in your room for I don't know how long. Then, all of a sudden, without saying a word, you take the car and stay out a whole evening. What's going on?"

I really don't want to tell her where I've been. It's like every time I do something I feel like doing, she prohibits it.

"Are you hiding something from me?" she asks.

"No."

Reluctantly I let go of the door and sit down. At some point in time, I'll have to tell her. I may as well get it over with now.

Mom gets a puzzled look on her face while I'm telling her about my evening.

"How did you come up with this?" she asks.

I don't know what I should answer. It's not just that I want to get away from home and do something different from what I'm used to. It's tough to talk about. We have never been accustomed to talking about what is going on inside us. In some way, I don't really know why I did this. I only know how lonely I feel, and that with each passing day I'm becoming more rigid, immobile and indifferent. I'm looking at Mom who sits up straight on her chair and looks me in the face. It will surely sound self-absorbed if I tell her how much boredom weighs on me and how empty I think my life is. The worst is that frightening sensation I have of being locked up in myself.

"Everything feels so boring and empty," I say.

"Don't you think that's your own fault?"

"For crying out loud," I say angrily, "is that really the only thing you can say? Of course, it's my own fault. What do you want me to do?"

I'm getting a crazy suspicion and sit up.

"Now, you're not starting to dig up the past, are you?"

She is beginning to drum on the armrests with her fingers.

"I can't understand where you get your weird ideas from."

I'm stiffening, and a slight redness rises into her cheeks. We are staring into each other's eyes. I'm so stunned and irate that I can't think. She slowly opens her lips.

"I'm sorry. What am I saying? I didn't mean it. We simply want to help you."

"You should have thought of that a bit sooner," I say and get up.

"I'm going to bed."

The weather has been wet for a few days, but tonight it is changing. From the kitchen comes the sound of a loud banging of pots.

"Could you tell me when they arrive?" yells Mom.

"Sure," I say.

I'm standing by the window and looking out at the fine snowflakes coming down at that moment, as they are hitting the sidewalk and the road.

"Here they come," I call out.

Mom is taking off her apron as she steps into the living room. She folds it over her arm and reaches her hands up to tie her kerchief.

"Boy, I'm just in time getting ready," she says and runs her fingers through her hair. "What do I look like?"

"Good enough," I say.

She has been cleaning the whole house for several days because we are expecting Dad's sister and her husband for a visit. Dad has holed himself up in the workshop in the basement so as not to be in the way, and I was sitting in my room when I didn't help her. Even if the door had been closed, I couldn't have avoided hearing the noise of the slamming doors and of Mom's voice as she was talking to herself. I can't understand why she and Dad keep inviting Jenny and Ole. It would of course be inconceivable not to invite them because they're family and because we have been to their place last. It looks like Mom is trying to hide it, but I can tell that she is nervous when she leans over and looks out the window.

The silver-colored car drives up to the curb, and Jenny climbs out. She is wearing a brown fur coat that reaches down to her knees. Her gray hair, in a page hairdo, falls down upon the fur, and she is wearing high-heeled shoes. A wind blast comes round the corner, and she hurries, bent over, across the pavement. On the other side of the car, Ole appears. He takes hold of his fluttering necktie and stuffs it inside his jacket, then he pushes a hat down on his head and follows his wife up to the house. Out in the hallway, Mom looks herself over in the mirror and pinches her lips together to smooth out the lipstick while she opens the door to the basement and calls down the stairs to Dad.

A little later we are sitting at the table set for lunch in the living room. Jenny picks up a knife but puts it down again right away. She carefully dries her fingertips and then the knife on a napkin.

"Your household help is too busy I guess," she says and smiles, "the knife handle is greasy."

"Oh no," says Mom and jumps up from her chair, "I'll see to it that you get a clean one."

Her hand is trembling lightly as she hands a new polished knife over the table to Jenny.

"In truth, there's never anything but trouble with household aides," says Jenny. "If I just think about what my bathroom looks like at times…"

"You know very well…" says Mom.

"Yes…"

Jenny smiles at her.

"No, nothing," says Mom and, head lowered, sits back down on her chair.

Although I've been through this many times before, I am still astounded at Jenny's impudence and at the greed with which Ole heaps food on his plate. When he has eaten the herring and chased it down with a few schnapps, he leans back and puts one hand on his belly.

"Ah…" he lets out.

He is sitting there for a moment, digesting, then he turns to me.

"You'll finish school by summer, right?" he asks. "What are your plans for the future?"

It is as if a vacuum were opening in my head. I don't feel like telling him that I don't have any plans for the future, and that I can't decide what to do when I graduate from high school. But what worries me is that I don't feel like doing anything.

"He's getting good grades," says Dad.

"Our son has just been appointed junior manager in his company," says Ole. "He is one of the youngest at that level."

I can feel my anger about his grossness grow. I say, "I've thought of going on welfare."

There is the sound of a half-choked cough, and Dad is holding a napkin over his mouth. He gets red spots on both cheeks. When he can speak again, he says, "I have thought that I may try to find him a position in a bank."

"I sure don't want to sit and count other people's money," I say angrily.

Mom lifts up a platter as she hastens to address Ole.

"No, just look," she says, "it's really awful how it's snowing."

We have gotten up from the table, and Jenny and Dad are standing by the window.

"Shouldn't we drive out to the farm?" she says. "I'd like to see how the buildings are holding up."

"The farm?" says Dad and starts laughing. "Do you mean the farm where we grew up? That's really nothing but a ruin I tell you."

"I'll just change my shoes," she says and frowns slightly.

We drive out on the roadway in the silver-colored car and turn onto a side street. On top of a hill sits the farm or, rather, what is left of it. Ole turns off the engine, and we step out into the loose, blowing snow. On the walls, partially collapsed, there are tufts of withered grass.

I'm still in the same antsy state of excitement as during lunch and walk in through the ruins to slip away from the others. The rage stays with me and is sitting inside me like an uneasy feeling of standing on the tip of a long pole and swaying back and forth. A large bird flies up, frightened, from the corner of what had once been the living room. It looks as if a messy pile of feathers and slapping wings were being tossed into my head, and I get down involuntarily on my knees, while the bird disappears, screeching loudly, over the nearby fallen wall. The surroundings are beginning to float out of my sight, and I blink my eyes, half in shock, to see clearly.

When I turn, there are Dad and Jenny facing each other in the former courtyard. She has her hands on her sides, and her hair flutters into her face. Dad looks different than earlier in the day. He resembles the man who stands and holds me in his arms in countless amateur photos taken shortly after I was born. Nevertheless, the image doesn't quite fit. Detached, incomprehensible words are carried to me by the wind, and I curiously move closer.

"You are a womanizer! You're growing a horn right out of your forehead," shouts Jenny. "You are bringing shame on the family!"

Mom is standing, with her back pressed against a wall, and watching Dad and Jenny with bulging eyes. All of a sudden, rage rises up in me, and I bit my lip, not to scream out loud. My hatred for Jenny is so strong that it feels like my heart will stop.

Dad turns around abruptly and walks in between two dilapidated walls. From the way he moves, I can tell he is angry.

In the former barn, he is standing in the farthest end and ls looking down on the ground. I step up close to give him a comforting pat on the shoulder.

"You mustn't feel bad about this," I want to say, "really, it's all my fault."

When I open my mouth, there's another voice talking.

"Dad, you are a pig. How do you think it's possible to live with the knowledge that I was conceived in sin? I am sin itself, dressed in flesh and blood."

Dad looks up and slowly starts walking in my direction. His mouth is twisted, and his eyes shine hatefully. I step back in surprise, and we follow each other step by step so that the distance between us grows neither bigger nor smaller. I bump into a wall and stand, unable to move, while he is coming closer. He grabs hold of the handles of an old, rusty wheelbarrow lying overturned on its side, and pushes it toward me. The moment the wheelbarrow bumps into my stomach, I scream, but without feeling any fear. I know that the wheelbarrow protects me rather than threatens me. Dad dares not come closer and meet me body to body. It is his blood in my veins that stops him.

On the way back, the mood in the car is almost cheerful as though the outing had, for some reason, cleared the air between Dad and Jenny. It's only me who feels uncomfortable. I don't know why I have the same feeling that I've done something wrong that I had when I was little. We are standing in a churchyard, and Jenny takes a heart made of moss that she had brought along out of the car trunk. I'm watching as she puts it down by the stone that stands on the grave of Grandma and Grandpa, and the only thing I can think of is that in the dirt below me lie two grinning skeletons.

"Are you coming back in?" asks Mom when we are again sitting in the car.

"No, thanks," says Jenny. "We would like to get home before it grows too dark, right, Ole?"

In the shade under the trees, the darkness is so solid that that I can only make out the dial of the watch on my wrist. I have seen from last time that it's worth coming early. Not likely any of the others have arrived yet.

When I open the door, I see that Louise is standing on one leg and is sticking the other into a pair of sweatpants.

"You sure come early," she says and smiles at me.

Indeed, nobody else is in the room.

She is sitting down on the floor and after I've taken off my coat, I'm sitting down too. In the silence that ensues suddenly we exchange a somewhat forced smile. I can't think of anything to say.

"Smile," she says, "you look so worried."

I try again to smile. She leans forward and opens a book with a speckled cover that is lying on the floor. I turn my face and look at a shadow, flickering slightly, that has caught my attention. Way back in the room there is a mysterious object that wasn't there last time, or that I didn't notice. It is made of a gold-colored metal, either brass or bronze, and on each side stands a white candle in a low white candleholder that looks like an open tilted flower. I can't see what the figure represents, and I pinch my eyes. It looks human and is standing on one leg in a large, jagged ring. It has four arms that each point in their own direction, and all are bent, just like the other leg. It looks as if it were dancing on the back of another figure that appears to be either a child or a demon. There is something alien and cruel about this whole object, which makes me curious and a little excited. It occurs to me that it must be an Indian god whose name I don't know.

As the silence becomes heavy, I feel relieved when the door opens, and the other participants start coming in, single or in pairs. Louise nods and smiles at each one in turn.

"She's fantastic, isn't she?" says a woman who follows me out to the cars.

The others are walking before and behind us.

"She really is," I say.

It feels surprisingly comfortable stepping from the room out into the cold night. We have done some exercises, standing up and lying on the floor, and I have an unaccustomed feeling in my body of elation and well-being.

"You can tell she has a strong radiance," I say.

"Yes," says the woman. "I have previously been to this kind of meeting. That voice, it's like, it gives me goosepimples."

We walk along the last bit of the path to the cars in silence. The woman opens the door and, as she is sitting down, she lifts her hand and calls out, "See you next week."

* * *

After the comfortable meeting last night, I spend the entire morning feeling that time is passing with unusual slowness. I don't know why the monotony of days affects me even more than it used to. Ever since I got up, I have had this sensation of not being there even though I fight it with all I have.

We are in biology class. For the past half-hour, Hansen who speaks with a sleepy, monotonous voice has been sitting at his desk with a pointer in one hand and a diagram in the other and talking about the development of earthworms. All around me the others have been busy writing small notes they push across the tables and hand back and forth between the rows.

Restless and distracted, I'm beginning to look around. The feeling of being responsible for everything has returned. On a shelf along one wall, there is a row of sealed glasses with snakes and amphibians in alcohol. After a brief moment looking at the pale, fetus-like bodies, I shudder and turn my gaze away. Nevertheless, the impression of my surroundings keeps creeping up on me. It's like I'm breathing it in through the air that has a slightly rotten and stuffy smell. Quite gradually I'm getting the feeling that I'm being surrounded and pushed in a corner. Cold sweat oozes from my palms and temples, and with an odd, spinning sensation in my body, like my arms and legs are asleep, it occurs to me that even if I don't want to, I can't help remembering the spit and the poisonous bacteria. It is as if a fracture happened. It must have been seven years ago. I shove my chair back, and stand up, nausea rising in my throat.

"Yes," says Hansen and looks at me, annoyed at being interrupted.

"I'd like to go to the restroom," I say and make a swallowing movement.

He nods briefly and keeps on talking.

I open the door to the bathroom across from the biology class, but it feels like entering a different one, just as clean and cold and covered with smooth white tiles. In a brief overwhelming flash, I recall how every recess, a few minutes before the bell rang, I would go to the secluded toilet way in the back of the schoolyard, to be by myself so that no one could see what I thought.

The light comes in from a small rectangular window way up in the outer wall. I go to the sink and open the faucet. My face that I can see in the mirror above the sink is pale, with little pearls of sweat on my upper lip and forehead. I bend down and am about to splash cold water over my face when I freeze. I notice that it isn't just water that is spiraling down in the drain. It's the toilet itself that causes me to feel repressed memories. Frightened, I take a step back, and my legs begin to tremble lightly.

To my side, on the cold tiled floor, stands a slender boy, his head bowed down and his arms hanging by his sides. At exactly the same moment, both of us turn around like mirror images and stare at each other. He cautiously looks up, and our eyes meet. I notice that my mouth is filling with spit, and I can't swallow it. The boy opens his mouth and lets the spit flow into his hand. With our first steps toward the sink, we run into one another. I am the boy who lifts his hand and pours the spit into the sink. The water comes slashing out of the faucet, and I can see, with fear and excitement, how the long threads of mucus are sliding down the drain where they settle in a tangled lump. I spit down into the sink, and I keep spitting until I can force no more saliva out between my lips. Then I carefully rub my gums and lips on my sleeve, and, when I'm certain that my mouth is dry, I scrub my hands with soap and turn off the faucet with a hard push with my elbow as I must have deposited bacteria on it when I turned it on. There is almost no place left I can be, because of spit, filth, and poisonous bacteria.

The bell rings, and after waiting a few minutes, I step out into the deserted schoolyard. I'm nauseated and dizzy with fear, but I walk down that narrow, institutionally painted hallway. I don't know why I can't swallow my spit. I only know that there is something I must do, otherwise the Earth will come to an end. I'm wiping my gums with my sleeve one more time while I'm carefully pushing open the door to the classroom, without using my hands, and then sneak to my seat. I nervously slide my tongue up against my palate and down along my gums, realizing that my mouth is still dry. I'm so relieved at that that I barely care about the voice speaking at the other end of the room or the words written on the blackboard. Small drops of mouth water are beginning to ooze out from between my teeth, and upset and terrified, I can feel my mouth slowly filling with spit. I force myself not to swallow.

My mouth is so full of saliva that it keeps running into my throat all the time. Nervously I put an open book upright on the table and lower my head behind it and peek out under my armpits. It doesn't look as though any of the others take notice of me. I let the spit ooze into my hand, and when it's filled up, I carefully reach it under my chair and pour the slimy liquid out on the floor. I dry my hand thoroughly on my pantleg and put it stiffly on my thigh, palm up. Then I sit up and make an effort to listen to the voice and follow it. I can feel how little drops of spit again keep slowly collecting in my mouth.

For many months, the guys in my class have waited for me every day in driveways and behind cars when I walk home from school. Some days there are only three or four of them, other times it's only Lars. He, however, waits for me every day. When the bell rings, I get up right away and, at the same moment, receive a hard push in the back so that I'm just about to fall down.

"We're waiting for you," shouts a voice, and I manage to catch a glimpse of Lars' stubby nose and his brown, short hair at the back of his neck before he disappears into the crowd heading out.

I remain standing behind, by myself, and I'm slowly packing my bag while I'm looking anxiously at the door. There is a whole lake of spit under my chair, but I try not to look down there. If I don't look at it, it's kind of as if it didn't exist. I spit into the sink by the blackboard and wash my hands carefully. When the last noise in the resounding hallway has died down, I cautiously venture out of the classroom.

I step out through the school gate and look in both directions. The street is deserted. I hardly dare believe my luck. I'm standing there for a moment and filling up with relief. Maybe, neither Lars nor the other guys are waiting for me today. But I expect that any moment they may show up, and just to be on the safe side, I'm picking up one of the detours I usually use to go home, while I'm always careful not to step on the cracks in the spaces between the pavement stones.

I've come down the street a bit when I spot the dark-haired head as Lars ducks down behind a car. I turn around and my heart starts pounding while I'm running back toward the school gate. The sound of steps is coming close the whole time, and suddenly I'm tossed forward so that I fall over my bag. Lars heavily lands on me, and I automatically put my arms over my head and begin to cry. The whole time I'm waiting to feel the blow and the knotted fists dig into my body.

Instead, I hear Lars' voice.

"Why are you so weird? Why do you pour your spit out on the floor?"

I produce a gurgling sound and draw closer to the ground to make myself invisible. I can hear what he says, but something doesn't make sense. There isn't anyone who knows that I pour out my spit. I'm so shocked that, at first, I don't notice that the weight of his body has lifted from my chest. I start crying still more violently, and I'm curling myself up, expecting to receive the kick from one of his shoes.

For a long time, nothing happens, then there is the weak sound of steps going away. I get up confused and look up and down the street. I can't believe that Lars has left without beating me up, but the street is empty. I wipe up the water from my cheeks. I'm waiting for him or the other guys to come running out from the driveways and to rise up from behind the cars. It's just to trick me that he's gone. I look at my clothes and discover that there are spots of dirt on them. I try to brush it off, but it won't come off, and that makes me shudder with fear of getting dirt on my hands. I'm just about to cry again. Dad may beat me if I come home with dirty clothes. I bend down and wipe away the dirt as well as I can.

I have picked up my bag and I'm just about to take a step forward when I discover that the stone in front of me is cracked. The crack looks like a black jagged mouth that can open any moment and devour me. I'm spitting with panic. There's no place where I can set down my foot without stepping on a line. I turn around and walk back and then down a different street. When I've walked down that one a bit, there is another cracked stone blocking my way. I stand stock-still and debate in my mind. Half wavering I take a step onto the asphalt. I don't dare look back and wait that any moment I'll be hit with punishment as the ground cracks under my feet.

I have come home, and I'm lying on my bed in my room with a book, but I'm so exhausted with anxiety that I don't have the strength to read it. The only thing I still have the strength for is pouring spit into my hand and drying my hand on my pantleg. It's been such a long time since I began this that I can't remember anymore when it was. Death, cancer, blood poisoning, the dangerous words that I mustn't think about if I want to avoid being infected keep cropping up in my head. I make a desperate effort not to think about them. It is nearly dark everywhere when I hear a noise up above my head. It sounds as if some creature is sitting inside the wall and breathing. It starts sizzling greatly behind the wallpaper, and a poisonous, invisible steam is slowly oozing out into the room. It's like my heart skips a beat and then stops beating altogether. I can't catch a breath any longer and start screaming. The air is poisonous, and I'm being strangled.

The door opens. Mom's silhouette shows against the electric light that comes in through the door opening.

"What's the matter? Stop already with the screaming."

My stomach contracts, like in a cramp, and I let out, involuntarily, another scream of fear.

"I can't cope with this any longer," she says back over her shoulder. "If you don't call the doctor, I will."

I can perceive the fear in her voice, and that makes me let out another scream.

She is leaning down over my bed and is shaking me while she whispers, "What's wrong? What's wrong?"

I'm lying on my bed, exhausted, my cheeks drained when the doctor arrives. I know him well. He is the same one who has always come to see me whenever I was sick.

"Ah, here he is. Listen, what's going on, young man?"

I shake my head desperately and look away.

"He can't speak because his mouth is full of saliva," says Mom, "he can't swallow it."

The doctor is standing there for a moment, then he says, "Go and fetch a glass of water."

Mom disappears into the kitchen and returns with a glass on a tray. The doctor takes the glass and hands it to me.

"Drink!"

Again, I shake my head. The doctor grabs the back of my neck and holds the glass against my lips.

"Try and drink a drop of the water."

He pours from the glass, and although I'm pressing my lips together, the water flows into my mouth. I cough and have to swallow to avoid getting sick. The doctor sets the glass back on the tray, and, terrified, I wonder if I'm still alive. It feels like I am.

"Now let me hear what's wrong."

I fearfully look up at Mom and Dad and over at the doctor.

"Why don't you want to swallow your saliva?"

I don't know. I only know that there is something I need to do or else the Earth comes to an end.

The doctor makes a few more attempts at getting me to talk. The whole time I have Mom's and Dad's frightened faces sitting on my retina. I'm sure they're worried about me.

"Let's go into the living room," says the doctor and lays his hand on Dad's arm.

From inside the living room, I can hear their voices. The doctor's sounds the darkest.

"Do you have a sense that he has been exposed to a trauma?"

"No," says Dad.

"Does he have problems in school?"

"He's always done well."

"He never tells us anything anymore," says Mom. Every afternoon he comes home and shuts himself up in his room and lies on his bed with a book. He doesn't go out into fresh air. It is as if he's completely gone. I can stand right by his bedside and talk to him, but he doesn't hear a word."

"What about the spit he won't swallow? How long has that been going on?"

"We don't know. But that's not all. He also washes his hands for the least reason. At least twenty to thirty times a day. His hands are all red and raw."

I curl up and turn my face to the wall.

"At night, we can hear him walking around in his room after we've gone to bed. He keeps saying he can't sleep because there are cracks in the ceiling. What can we do?"

"How old is he?" asks the doctor.

"Eleven years."

At night, when I have gone to bed, Dad comes into my room with a glass of water in one hand. He has something in his other hand that I can't see. He is sitting down by my bedside, and I hurriedly pull up the blanket to hide the wet spot on the sheet where I poured out the spit.

"Now you'll see," he says and shows me what he has in his hand. "Here are a few pills we got for you from the doctor. This one is a nerve pill."

He pushes one of the two small white pills with his finger.

"And this is a sleeping pill. This way you won't need to be admitted. We would have to end up hospitalizing you, I tell you, and you don't want that, right?"

I'm looking down at the two little white pills with the strange names. They look harmless. They look like those drops I sometimes buy in the candy store.

"No," I say, "but there's a crack in the ceiling."

There is also a creepy eye looking down on me, but I don't dare tell him that. I know that he won't believe me. But I need to talk about it.

"Where?" he asks and looks up. "I can't see any crack."

"But yes, right there in the corner."

"There's a line in the ceiling tile."

I shut up, but I can clearly see the crack and the eye.

"Swallow the pills, so you get better. You do want to be healthy, don't you?"

"Sure I do."

Dad pets me on my hair while I am obediently swallowing the pills.

A little later, when he thinks I'm sleeping, he gets up and quietly pulls the door shut. I open my eyes and stare at the crack in the ceiling. The vicious, silvery eye is looking down at me.

I am getting a weird sensation of growing heavy in my body, and it feels like my eyelids are going to close on their own the whole time. But I'm still wide awake. I'm beginning to draw labored breaths. I feel that the sleep that's coming is not natural sleep, but a slow stealthy poison. I'm diving into it, but then abruptly wake up again. I raise myself and sit up and roll my eyes. My heart is pounding hard and anxiously. It feels as if something unknown and dangerous has invaded my body. I start fighting sleep as hard as I can. I am more fearful than I have ever been, and in a curiously lucid manner I understand that I'm captured and can't escape. The dangerous poison is in my body.

The water pipes have stopped humming as I cautiously slide out of my bed. I climb up on the table in the kitchen and open the uppermost cupboard door. On the middle shelf are the two medication bottles with my name on them. Without making the least noise, I'm sneaking out to the bathroom and pour the pills into the toilet. The relief at watching them disappear is so strong that I'm just about to cry. Then I spit into the sink, rinse my mouth and carefully wash my hands.

The rest of the night I'm lying terrified and fighting not to fall asleep while I'm staring at that vicious eye that slightly glows, like silver, in the dark. I dare not think about what will happen when Mom and Dad discover early tomorrow that I've thrown out the pills. But I must not fall asleep. I must never again take those poisonous pills. If I make a mistake, the Earth will end.

"Where have you been?"

I look up and see in the mirror that Hansen has come into the restroom and is standing there with one hand on the door.

"It's been a long time since you went to the bathroom. We thought that something had happened."

"I…"

My voice fails me.

I clear my throat, raise myself up and try to make my voice sound calm and controlled.

"I'm coming," I say.

When he has gone back to the classroom, I go into the toilet stall and lock the door. I'm sitting down on the commode and pull my legs up under myself.

Part 2

The sun is shining down from a sky that is cloudless and almost ironically blue. The window stands open, and though I only wear a t-shirt and shorts, I'm sweating so much that my thighs stick to the seat. It's been fourteen days since we went on break.

Mom steps through the door.

"Have you noticed how good the weather is?" she asks. "You haven't been outdoors for three days. Shouldn't you get some fresh air?"

She remains standing in the doorway, drying her wet hands on her apron.

"I don't have time for that," I say and close the book I'm reading. I turn my overworked eyes in her direction.

"I'm still catching up on reading that and that and that," I say and point at the piles of books lying on my desk and on the floor.

I have a feeling that I'm going crazy from reading. Last night I started hearing a sound, a whistling tone, that filled the room. It slowly dawned on me that it was the background noise of the television, turned on, that Mom and Dad were watching in the living room on the other side of the wall. I have heard that dogs can go insane from sounds but not that it could happen to humans, and I was frightened. I'm afraid that, if I don't watch out, my obsessive thoughts will return.

It doesn't appear as though Mom has heard what I said. She is looking around in the room and getting a definite twitch around her mouth.

"You should get this cleaned up," she says. "It's overflowing with papers and books everywhere."

"I'm studying for my exam," I say, "will you please go so I can continue?"

"You won't order me around," she says.

"You mustn't tell me all the time what I'm supposed to do," I say.

Mom takes a step back and clenches her hands in the apron pockets.

"It might be better if you listened to us and trusted more in God and tore yourself away from that broad, Louise."

43

Just as I get ready to answer, she has turned and closed the door hard after herself.

The heat is still lying in the streets, even though it's after seven o'clock. Dad was absolutely insistent that I go and get outdoors, and at long last I gave in. We are walking down a side street and come to a meadow that sits in the vicinity of the house. It's been five days since I was last outside, and I feel weak in my knees, like a convalescent up for the first time.

"There's something I'd like to talk to you about," says Dad.

He is holding down the uppermost wire of the electric fence with his handkerchief so as not to get shocked, and we clamber over it. We are walking under the trees lining the fence and continuing on that way.

"I don't mean to push you," he says. "I know full well that it's not for our sake that you are taking that exam, but…we naturally have certain expectations of you. Don't you think it's about time that you find out what way you'll be going afterwards…you can't keep treading water here."

"I'm just on break," I say, "the vacation hasn't started yet."

I shoot a glance at him. He has begun to hunch over and look old.

I know that he has always done what was expected of him. When he was young, he would have liked to work with numbers and accounting—something that, to his disappointment, did not interest me in the least—but it was impossible for him to realize that. He couldn't afford to get an education. It was more important for him to find work so he could earn money and thus provide for a family. Mom claims that that was the reason he got married so late.

I feel sure that, even if he tried, he wouldn't be able to understand me. I'm not even sure I understand myself.

He is looking over at me.

"If you want to know," I say, "I have thought of taking a few months off, and…I don't want to study again."

In view of his facial expression, I say:

"It is as if everything is planned in advance. I know what will be happening, day in, day out, many years down the line. I want something different to happen. I think…I have a feeling that I need time."

"What would you like to happen?" He asks.

I'm silent. I don't know.

"This way you're not getting anywhere, you know," he says and furrows his forehead worriedly. "You can't get around the necessity that you get an education and work for a salary and come out ahead. Are you sure I shouldn't try and get you a job in a bank?"

"It's you who would like to work in a bank," I say. "I don't want to."

Louise is down on her knees and lighting the two candles on each side of the Indian statue.

"Good evening," she says and turns her head.

She blows out the match and gets up. The electric light that streams down from the ceiling makes her hair shine and appear transparent at the top. She sits down on the floor, and I sit down across from her.

I can't stop wondering how strange it is that, when you have seen a face enough times, you begin to think you know that person even if it isn't necessarily true. It occurs to me that, although I have come here once a week for half a year, I barely know Louise.

"Are things going well with your exam?" she asks and smiles.

"Yes," I say, "we're done with most subjects. We're finishing up in three days."

"Did you pass?"

I nod and smile.

"Good luck. What will you do when you're finished?"

"I don't know," I admit.

"Yes," says Louise, "it's hard to have to take responsibility for one's own life if one isn't used to freedom. I think it's the way we're raised that is wrong. We don't appreciate maturity."

I'm thinking about what she has said. I'd never looked at it that way.

"How is it going with your exercises?" she asks and turns her face away from the light.

"Good. I practice almost every day."

"That sounds great, I tell you," she says.

I stretch out one of my legs and pull myself forward with my arms until my forehead touches my kneecap.

"Remarkable! You couldn't do that before, right?"

I lift my head and smile.

"I can't understand why you're always so cautious," she says. "You don't have any reason at all for that."

Her words embarrass me and I'm relieved to see that the other participants are beginning to come in through the door. Louise greets everyone, and I nod at the two or three I've exchanged a few words with. The chitchat ends after they find their spots. Louise glances around the circle. She lets her chin sink down on her chest and sits motionless.

"Yes," she says and sits up, "as you know, this is the last time before summer vacation."

I'm moving uneasily. I'm trying not to think of that.

She smiles and pushes her chin forward:

"Before we get started, I have to tell you something I experienced today. In the past weeks, I've been busy planning and arranging the courses I give over the summer vacation, and two weeks ago I went to the doctor to be examined, because I felt exhausted, far too exhausted for it to seem normal. I had begun to think it was something psychosomatic. In the morning, I was up to get my test results. You can't guess what the doctor said…"

She pauses, and a twitching goes across her face.

"It is something that comes with age. That's what he said, so help me God. I'm only forty-three years old… I simply don't want to deal with that. No doctor shall get me to believe that it is normal to feel tired because you grow older. Think of the wild animals that live in nature. They don't get sick or grow old but retain their vitality until they die. Health is not only a question of not having any symptoms of an illness. I said so to the doctor, right to his face, but of course, he wouldn't listen to me. I can get quite upset when I imagine that it's this kind of people who are supposed to be in charge of our health."

She pulls her legs up against her chest and wraps her arms around her knees.

"That's like something I could have said," says a woman, Ingrid, who is sitting straight across from me. "I don't believe either all the nonsense they are telling us. No one will come and tell me how to live my life. I drink that booze and smoke all the cigarettes I want to."

Louise looks surprised, then she starts laughing.

"We may as well get going," she says, and her face becomes serious.

She turns her sight toward me.

"Can't you come up to the floor and show us that exercise you did before?"

"Me?" I ask.

"Yes."

I get up embarrassed and step out to the floor where I sit down. I lay my forehead against my kneecap and notice that the pain from the sinews in my leg nearly makes me see black before my eyes. When I look up, Louise's gaze is resting on me. She is smiling with appreciation.

"He practices every day," she says. "It is not a question of overdoing it occasionally. It's that regular training that yields results."

It's the end of the evening, and we are lying in the dark on the floor.

"And now," says Louise, "you're on your way into a state where you are neither asleep nor awake. It's like a dream, but it is something else. Does that sound complicated? I myself am always thinking about the difference between inspiration and fantasy."

It is as if I am getting firm ground under my feet. I discover, as I have done at other times we did the exercise, that, without moving, I can look down on my own body as if I were in two places at the same time. I'm standing on a planet of metal. Everything seems distant and unreal, but simultaneously present and close, like I'm using a different kind of sense than the one we usually use. It feels as though a number of insights come to me out of nothing. They are there in advance. Although I cannot overview the planet, I know it's round and flat like a wheel and, on its underside, dark and lifeless like the backside of the moon. The feeling it gives me standing on the planet may be like the one you get when you return to a place where you'd been happy, but I have never been here before.

Way out in space I can see the globe which hovers in a blue fog. The body I'm standing on must be one of those never seen yet in an astronomic observatory. Its surface is shining gold and as hard as metal. I stoop down and let my hand slide over the surface and collect a little pile of dust in my palm. The dust is unusually heavy, and I get all excited as I realize that it's gold.

A little ahead of me there is a cluster of trees and a thicket of bushes, all of crystal. High up in the crystal trees sits a flock of speckled birds. Farther away a group of gazelles graze on a plain of silver, and way out at the limit of my line of sight there is a row of gilded mountains. A river of quicksilver streams down over the rocks and splashes, in a perfect arc, into the nearly motionless surface.

The trunks and branches of the trees and bushes are shining like thousands of rainbows in the sun. Every time one of the small hot winds causes the glass leaf to move, it emits a sharp, quivering sound that keeps climbing in pitch until it suddenly disappears. From the branches, there hang large clusters of red, golden and blue fruits that resemble precious stones, ruby, topaz and sapphire.

I set myself to picking precious stone fruit and fill my pockets with them. To my surprise I suddenly see that I'm surrounded by people who are stepping out of cracks in the air. Their skin is golden, and their hair is blue-black. They are tall and slim and very straight, with proudly raised heads. Through the airy fabric their costumes are made of, I can see that they are created the same way as we are. They are not hostile as I fear for a moment but surround me in a friendly manner and stretch out their hands to touch my skin, my hair and my clothes, while they are talking among themselves in an incomprehensible language in bright voices that like birds' twitter. They appear innocuous and make me think of elves dancing round in a chain dance during a moon-lit night in the dew on a meadow.

Some of the people pick gemstones and eat them while others are running around, playing and laughing, like children in their light, transparent robes. All of a sudden I discover that several of them, using a single small ledge, jump up into the air and start floating around while flapping their arms and legs to move forward. It doesn't look like they have wings, but their clothes flutter so much that I'm not sure. Their wings may be invisible. I keep watching the flying people, wondering how gravity can work on this planet. Perhaps it's not as strong as down on Earth.

I'd like to find out if I also can fly, but I'm so overwhelmed by all the new impressions that I don't dare to throw myself up into the air to see if it can carry me, out of fear that it might completely turn upside down my sense of reality. Instead, I turn and begin to walk down toward the quicksilver lake where a few naked, long-limbed women are bathing.

While I'm walking to the lake, I catch sight of a woman who, all by herself, is squatting in a secluded cleft between two metal rocks. Suddenly, she cries out weakly, and an egg, the size of a child's head, falls down between her legs. She stands up and, leaning forward, is looking at the egg. Then she sits down right there, with a distant, dreamy expression on her face. I have a sensation of seeing something I'm not meant to see, and I hurriedly go on my way.

At the shore of the quicksilver lake, I stop and lift my eyes toward the sun that sits above the highest of the gilded mountains. The sun is uncommonly strong and looks like it's twice as big as when seen from Earth. It hurts my eyes to stare directly into its light. I close my eyes, but a circle of flames is remaining on my retina with undiminished intensity. I can sense that the light burns itself into my skin, and it feels as if my blood pulsates more strongly through my blood vessels. It's like I'm feeling more alive than…

"Wake up slowly," says Louise in a low voice, softly and a little hoarse.

That is an uncomfortable moment, like I'm floating weightless in the room. I note how emptiness sucks through my chest, and I try to get a hold of myself. I can barely stand the thought that the beautiful metal world has disappeared.

For a little while longer, I am feeling weightless, but then I feel the hard pressure of the floorboards under my back.

A murmur is spreading through the room. I open my eyes, but I feel so far out of it that some minutes pass before I sit up. Around me are the others, pulling at their unremarkable clothes, and out on the floor there sits Louise.

"Looks like you were very far away," she says.

I nod, still way out of it. Then I pull myself together and, with a jump, stand upright on my legs. I go on to put on my clothes like the others.

They start slowly moving toward the exit. Louise is standing by the door and shaking hands.

"Have a good summer," she says. "I hope we meet again."

I remain standing by the wall and fumble with a button, and by and by it comes so that Louise and I alone are left. Though I've known all evening that it's the last time, it's like it only now really sinks in. I have a sense that everything is winding down.

"What an evening!" she cries out. "Did you notice that there were two who fell asleep during the last exercise?"

"No," I say, "I didn't hear that."

She laughs and comes over to me.

"It was just so that they were snoring. Well, they may well have been tired. I know well that I'm being unfair," she says. "I'm just a bit irritable this evening. It must be that visit to the doctor."

She turns off the light and we step out into the entryway.

"I'll get busy on the farm," she says. "Will you keep on with the exercises even while we're on break?"

"Yes," I say.

I'm feeling sad as she shakes hands with me to say goodbye.

"Maybe we'll see each other again after the summer vacation," she says.

"Yes," I say.

She closes the door and I step out onto the courtyard under the night sky.

It's been several hours since we ate, and from the corner where I'm standing, I can just barely make out the contours of the others through the thick cigarette smoke. It's been a long time since the electric light was turned off, and although all the windows are open, so that the music pounds rhythmically down on the gardens in the neighborhood, and the candles on the tables flicker in the draft, it is still so warm that I'm feeling uncomfortable. Most of the girls wear white summer dresses that make their sunburned skin look even browner. When we arrived, the guys wore dark suits with white shirts and neckties. By now, they've cast off the jackets and ties and unbuttoned the shirts at the neck. Almost all of them, just like me, wear student caps. I drink a little cold white wine from the glass I'm holding in my hand, and I'm drying the sweat off my forehead.

I stiffen a bit when I discover that Hans and Helle are on their way in my direction. She has laid one arm round his neck, and it looks like they're supporting each other to keep from falling.

"Is that you standing there?" asks Helle and looks me up and down.

I don't answer. She can obviously see me.

"Aren't you glad we're done?"

Just as I'm coming up with an answer, Hans is pulling at her arm impatiently, and they walk on to one of the other rooms.

Out on the floor where it's cleared, five or six couples are dancing with big movements of their arms and stiff, uncertain steps. Their voices and unnaturally loud laughter reach me during pauses in the music and every time CDs are changed.

One of the couples is Lars and Vibeke. She is the girl I've secretly been in love with, but I'd never have dared to come close to her.

I start feeling awkward standing in the corner. My face feels stiff even though I try to look natural and relaxed. I'm making my way across the dance floor and step out onto the terrace. It's been a while since darkness has fallen, and the air is comfortably cool.

I lean against the metal railing and look down into the garden. Dew has fallen, and the freshly mown lawn gives off a strong pleasant odor. I have the sense that it's tonight that I will take stock, think about my past and future, but it seems like there's nothing to take stock of. I'm glad to be done, but the future worries me.

Where will I go? It is as if I've lost something I can't get back. I have a weird sensation up under my ribs. It feels like something sharp, hard, and cold is lodged in there. I bend down over the railing and sniff at my arm: It smells a little of salt and sweat.

The past days, after we finished the exam, I've been spending time at the beach where I found a deserted spot. I've been lying in the strong sun and feeling nearly desperate with loneliness, but, at the same time, I've been trying to avoid other people. After the quiet days, the noise from the music and the many people tonight are getting to me. I turn my head and look at the others through the window. If I'm going to stay here all night, I think I need to get drunk. I can no longer stand being out here by myself. I go back inside and edge along the wall to the kitchen. So as not to waste time unnecessarily, I leave the refrigerator door open and drink four of five beers while the light from the refrigerator casts a white, unnatural sliver of light on my face. I feel like forgetting it all, the uncertainty, the thoughts about what I'm going to do.

My tummy feels heavy and swollen and I can feel I'm getting drunk. I look down at the open refrigerator that hums loudly. I'm laughing and, out of a sudden feeling of tenderness, I put my arms around the refrigerator and press my cheek against its cold, white-painted surface. I try to imagine what the refrigerator looks like on the inside when its door is closed. Then I have an idea and raise my head. I slam the door shut and open it again so the light streams out. I laugh lightly, deep in my throat, and I open and close the refrigerator several times in a row. The exact same thing happens every time.

"I'll end up hitting you," I giggle drunkenly.

There is no doubt that the light goes out the moment I close the door.

It looks like I can't outfox the refrigerator, No matter how quickly I pull the door open, the light has already come on. If I want to solve the puzzle, I must go at it a different way. I decisively throw all food containers, wine bottles, the remaining beer bottles, and rows of shelving on the floor. Then I step into the refrigerator and squat down, my legs pressed up against my chest, and carefully pull the door shut. There is the sound of a click, and it turns dark around me.

"You can't fool me," I whisper and laugh, "your secret has been revealed."

A weak humming sound from the motor comes up slowly from between my legs, and they are beginning to fall asleep. I notice that the cold is moving in under my skin, and my teeth are beginning to chatter. Then the door is opened, and Vibeke stares in on me.

"What in the world are you doing inside the refrigerator?" she asks.

I'm feeling so embarrassed that it's her who opened the refrigerator that I stay in my position, huddled over, and blink my eyes toward the light. She has small pearls of sweat on her upper lip, and her sun-bleached hair hangs damply down over her cheeks. Behind her, in the open door, there are some of the others, looking back and forth in puzzlement between me and the messy pile of food items and bottles on the floor. I start laughing and, all of a sudden, I don't care at all what they are thinking. As I step out onto the floor, I notice how a vein starts throbbing in my forehead. I can't think of a time I ever felt so sure of myself. I must be more drunk than I think.

My voice sounds strange, like it's someone else who asks: "Should we dance?"

Vibeke looks at me in surprise, then she nods and takes the hand I stretch out to her.

The bedroom is dark, and it seems to be empty. I'm not sure what time it is, but it must be late. I must have danced a lot because I'm sweating so much that the sweat is running down my body. I must also have kept on drinking because I can't remember what happened after I came out of the refrigerator. I wipe the sweat off my forehead with the back of my hand and close the door behind me.

"What do you want?" says a voice.

I can't help being startled and turn my upper body in the direction the voice came from. I didn't think anybody else was in the room, and I almost expect to see a ghost.

In the weak gray light that comes in through the window, there sits Lars on one of the beds, half hidden behind a closet. His shirt is unbuttoned and hangs out over his pants, and under his student cap that he has pushed onto the back of his neck, his short brown hair is sticking out. He has a sullen, off-putting expression on his face. It looks like he's waiting for someone, and I am disturbing him.

"Is that you?" I ask in surprise and sit down at the foot end of the bed. "What are you doing here?"

"Beat it," he says, "I won't bother talking to you."

I try to hold back my hatred, but it is like heat that rises up in me and causes me to see white dots in front of my eyes. The vein is beginning to pound violently in my forehead. I hate the sight of him. I hate the sight of his angry, off-putting facial expression, which signals that he believes he can get away with what he wants with me. I hate him for what he's done to me, going after me in the streets, the embankments, the daily fear of what would happen on my way home. I can't understand how I could have been so unlucky to be going to the same grade, the same school as him. He is the guy who always did well and was popular. He is like a condensed point of evil in the darkness.

I'm leaning back. The vein is pounding and pulsating. The bed is waving slightly, like a boat. I feel very drunk. Suddenly I'm about to cry.

"Do you remember when I couldn't swallow my spit and poured it out on the floor?" I say. "Do you remember the day you sat on my back and asked why I was weird? Do you remember that you and the other guys always stood ready outside the school gate to beat me up? Why did you do that?"

I can hear myself talking and talking. I have a slight, alarming notion that I'm doing something embarrassing, but it's like I can't stop myself talking. It occurs to me that I'm doing the worst I can imagine.

He leans his head back and it seems as if he has sunk farther into the darkness. He doesn't say anything, and I keep staring at him until he looks down, a bit red in the face. Suddenly my anger is gone, and I get a strange feeling of compassion for him. Maybe he has regretted how he went after me. If only he'd talk to me like I was an ordinary sensible human being, I'd forgive him. It doesn't matter anymore. Perhaps, he'll talk if I shut up.

"You're nuts," he says.

At the sound of the door opening, we both turn our heads. Silhouetted against the light from the hallway, there stands Vibeke in the door opening. She closes the door and sits down on the bed and looks at each of us in turn.

"What's going on here?" she asks. "Am I missing out on something?"

Lars slowly turns to me.

"You may as well go now," he says.

"No," I say even though I can feel that I'm in the way. The thought that it was maybe her he'd been waiting for makes me still more upset and angry. I don't know what's going on with me. Lars sits up and stretches out his arm and puts it on her shoulder. I'm not as calm as I let on, but I'm staring into his eyes, and I put my arm around her hip. Vibeke is sitting there without moving. Lars and I keep staring into each other's eyes over her head.

"Tell me what you guys are up to," she asks and laughs uncertainly.

"Scram," says Lars, "can't you see you're in the way?"

I remain seated, not saying anything.

"You're way out of line," he says.

He gets up and walks to the door. For a moment, I think he's going to leave the room, then I hear that he turns the key in the lock. The weak crunching of the key as it turns gives me the uncomfortable sensation of something tightening, of being blocked inside. It's as if I can't catch my breath. I take my arm off Vibeke.

Lars takes hold of her arms and tries to push her down on the bed.

"Let go," she says, "not now."

"Didn't you hear what she said?" I say.

I still can't figure their relationship, but I'm sure I can hear anxiety in her voice.

I'm sitting like an onlooker and watch as he puts his hands on her thigh and lets them slide up under her dress.

Vibeke is lying halfway down on the bed on her elbows and is fighting with Lars, and her voice sounds loud and strained.

"Let go," she says, "unlock the door."

He is sitting astride her, holding her arms up over her head.

"Didn't you hear what she said?" I repeat.

I grab his shoulder and pull him back over. I can't stand watching this. I'm sure he's trying to rape her. Lars turns his upper body and takes hold of my arm. Vibeke wriggles free from under him, and he turns round on the bed. He hits my chin with a fist, and I feel a surprising pain as my head is pushed back. I gasp and sit up and try to kick him in the stomach. He crouches, then he jumps and falls heavily down on me. He presses my head over backward, and with heaving, excited breaths we set to fighting. I can't catch my breath, but I notice that Vibeke has opened the door, and that she is yelling out into the hallway.

The ceiling light is switched on, and the others come running and stop inside the door. Their voices are loud and scared.

"What's going on there?" exclaims a voice.

"Get them to lay off," yells another voice, "that will end with them beating each other to death. Get them to lay off."

54

With a strong pull Lars and I are being separated. Two pairs of hands are holding my arms fast to my back. Two of the other guys are holding Lars.

"I hate you," I say and try to kick him in the legs.

Lars pinches his eyes together and narrows his lips, then he looks away with an expression of discomfort on his face.

"What happened there?" asks a voice.

None of us replies. In the quiet, Vibeke starts crying.

"I hate all of you," I say.

I jerk my arms, and Erik and Thomas who held me let go.

Those standing in the door opening step aside, and I come out into the hallway in a daze. It's empty in the room where the music is playing softly. On the tables and on the floor, there are full ashtrays and empty and half-empty beer and wine bottles among the candles. In the entry hall, I take my jacket down from the clothes rack. Then I open the main door and step out onto the staircase.

The night is like a large shadow from outer space that falls down over me. I'm walking along a broken milky way, dotted, white stripes on the asphalt. At the right spot, I stand still and breathe a bunch of stars deep into my lungs. Then I take the stairs in long strides and put the key noiselessly into the lock.

"Is that you?" calls Mom from inside the bedroom.

The bed squeaks as she turns.

"Yes," I answer and feel my way forward through the hallway so that I don't bump into the low table standing against the wall.

While I'm standing at the toilet and brushing my teeth, my face begins to dissolve in the mirror. I'm nauseated from the excitement of tonight's events and I lean over the toilet bowl to throw up.

Though I'm tired and in a daze, I can't fall asleep. I twist and turn restlessly on the bed sheet. I hear a door open, and the sound of a water faucet being turned and, afterwards, the splashing of water as it runs into a glass. Then it's quiet while Mom is swallowing the water. She is talking to herself in a low voice while she is passing by my door on her way back. The bedroom door is closed again. I try to divert my thoughts, but they keep circling round a certain thing, and eventually I give in.

While I'm reaching a hand down toward my crotch, I see, to my surprise, that a picture of Vibeke, in the nude, turns up in my head. For a little while, she is standing in front of me in the dark. Then I slide off into an uneasy doze.

I start falling, and I push open a swinging door with my hand, into a hall from where the sound of music, laughter and loud voices comes out to me. The hall I find myself in is dark except for the bar and the stage which are lit up by a spotlight that is so powerful that it hurts my eyes when I look directly into it. Half hidden behind some screens with Chinese motives on them, there lies the dance floor where some human bodies are moving out of sync with their heads and arms and legs, like on a flickering incoherent picture. I sit down on a chair at the bar and look over at them.

While my eyes are gliding from couple to couple, I'm getting an astonishing vision that slowly grows stronger. I no longer see these couples as people who have who have met each other in this place, on this evening. It is as though an almost animalistic savagery had busted all bounds, and the faces, which no longer look like faces, reflect in every way the same passion and excitement. Of the human body, only two parts are left, two organs, which, however, have grown so large that they completely fill the remaining space. It appears as if the dancefloor were transformed into an arena for grotesque lust, where a distended vulva and a colossal penis are moving forth toward dissolution in a deep, bumping rhythm.

There sounds a bang, and a cloud of steam billows up from the stage. At the same time, one of the Chinese screens falls over with a clatter like it's hit by air pressure. A few women scream, and a man rises from the screen so that it looks in the confusion as if he's a part of the decorative pattern that's come alive. He's wearing a gold- and silver-hued costume that is laced and open in the crotch. With great thrusts of his hips, he wriggles forward toward the stage where a row of girls and young men have been dancing. The man moves into the center of the light and bends over, with his back toward us, like he wants to showcase a kind of rear face that is just as obscene as the dissolved faces down on the dancefloor. Some women squeal, and the laughter produces an echo from the walls.

I'm looking around with an unsettling feeling, and my eyes fall on a woman sitting at the far end of the bar.

She is the most beautiful woman I've ever seen and I notice that the short hairs on my arms and on the back of my neck stand up.

I'm studying her face thoroughly, and, feeling like I'm about to fall, I shove the bar stool aside and walk uncertainly over to her place.

"May I sit down?" I ask, and I can hear that I almost stammer.

"No," she says and lets a red-lacquered fingernail slide down the stem of her wineglass while simultaneously sending me a blurred and, at the same time, penetrating glance that makes me feel like air.

"Why do people always have to bother me?" she asks and moves her hand as if to wave me away along with the smoke from her cigarette.

I remain standing and wait. She stares in front of her with a tired expression on her mouth.

"I'm sure we'll meet again," I say.

I wake up as Mom is standing, leaning over me.

"Do you have any idea what time it is?" she asks. "It's after twelve."

I have headaches and blurred vision. The bright light hurts my eyes so bad that I can't focus on her.

"Was it a good party?"

My head is pounding, and the bedsheets are clammy with sweat from my body.

"Yes," I say, "it was fine."

"You didn't drink, did you?"

She is leaning over me and sniffs.

"No."

"Why don't you get up already? Are you sick?"

"Maybe I'm getting the…the…flu," I stammer.

Mom lays her hand on my forehead.

"You're pretty warm. Maybe you have a fever? Are you sure there is nothing going on here? Are you sure you had nothing to drink?"

"Yes," I say.

When she's gone, I come to think about what happened. I turn my face under the pillow and start laughing.

"Damn it, damn it," I moan with embarrassment as more and more details of last night come up in my memory. I can't stand thinking about how I acted. I'm trying to imagine how Vibeke is doing. I hope she's not feeling overly insulted.

Then I'm thinking that I will never again see Vibeke or Lars or any of the others. I'm sitting up in my bed.

* * *

The summer had been unusually warm, and I have just come back from the beach. I've flushed the sand and the salt water off me, and I'm sitting in an armchair in the living room, one leg dangling over the armrest. I had no idea that a summer day could be this long when there's nothing to do, and it has begun to get on my nerves. Realistically I don't have any idea at all what I should get on with. I've begun to regret my decision to do nothing all summer. It's of course not true, but I have the feeling that I've read all books once or twice.

The phone starts ringing. I get up and lift the receiver.

"Hello," I say.

"Hello," says a voice I'm so unprepared for that I'm repeating myself: "Hello."

"Yes, hello," says Louise, "are you there?"

"Yes," I say, "I was just so surprised."

"Now, listen. I'm calling to ask what you'll be doing the next few weeks."

"Nothing."

"Could you see yourself coming out here and staying? I have a course starting tomorrow, and I think you would get a lot out of participating."

"Yes," I answer, feeling overwhelmed.

For some reason or other, my heart starts pounding.

"It's kind of you to invite me, but isn't that expensive?"

"Don't worry about that," she says. "I'd like to invite you for a stay free-of-charge."

I'm standing there with the receiver in my hand, not saying anything. I can't understand what has made her invite me.

Then I say, "Yes, I'd love to."

Louise begins talking about some practical matters, but I'm still so surprised that I hear hardly anything.

"So, you'll come tomorrow."

"Yes."

We say goodbye, and I hang up, but I keep standing there, my hand on the phone. I have a hard time believing this.

Mom is sitting in the shade under a tree, her dress rolled up over her knees and legs stretched out in the sun. Dad is sitting right behind her, with a straw hat pulled down over his forehead.

"Louise just called," I say and squat down in front of them. "She has invited me to come out and stay on the farm."

"That was nice of her," says Dad.

"Has she invited you?" asks Mom in surprise and takes off her sunglasses. "How much will you have to pay for that?"

"Nothing. She's invited me to a free stay. I'll go out there tomorrow if I'm allowed."

"I don't understand what you get out of that broad," she says. "Do you actually know what's going on there? I really thought that was over."

I don't say anything so that we won't end up quarreling.

"You do exactly what you feel like doing, don't you?" she says. "What about starting to think about your future instead?"

"Let him decide," says Dad, "let him do as he likes."

* * *

"I just hope that we'll recognize you again when you come back," says Dad. "This is the first time, you know, that you're away from home for so long."

I'm standing at the curb, watching Dad turn the car around. He honks, and I wave goodbye. I've already noticed that Louise's car isn't parked in the driveway, which makes me wonder. I pick up my suitcase and walk across the lawn toward the farmhouse. The white walls are shining very bright in the sunlight, and a bit beyond them, I can see the white dunes by the sea.

I still have a hard time understanding the abrupt change that has occurred, and that I've been so lucky. Why is it me Louise has invited and not someone else from the group? I'm trying not to think about Mom's anger about my leaving.

I knock on the door, but no one opens it. Maybe no one is home? Maybe I've arrived too early? The door opens as I press the door handle down, and I step into the entryway where the staircase to the first meeting room is. The room where we used to practice is empty, and I open the door at the opposite end, leading to the part of the house I don't know. I step into a room that is empty too, then continue on into a large kitchen and a utility room where there is another door out into the courtyard. It looks like nobody is home. I'm beginning to wonder if I got the days mixed up. Was it only tomorrow that I was supposed to come? I walk back to the other room.

"Is anyone here?" I call out, semi-loud.

In an adjacent room, there's still another door I haven't tried yet.

I knock, and, when no one answers, I cautiously open the door and stop, surprised, on the doorstep. On a table sits a man with closed eyes. He has a strangely peaceful or remote expression on his face and smooth features, like a child. I shouldn't have entered, but it is too late to retreat. I remain standing and wait for him to open his eyes.

His upper body is bare, and he is wearing a pair of well-worn blue jeans. His body is lean, and his chest strong and well-trained. He has an angular face with a high forehead, and his hair hangs halfway down over his shoulder.

"Excuse me," I say quietly and clear my throat.

He opens his eyes, but still has an absent expression on his face. Then he turns his gaze toward me, and awareness comes back into his eyes.

"Good morning," I say and shift my weight from one leg to the other. "I'm sorry I just walked in on you like this, but I'm looking for Louise. She's invited me to a course."

* * *

He climbs down from the table, and he's uncommonly tall when he straightens up. "Is that you? Good morning. Louise told me that you would come," he says. "I'm Louise's husband…Joakim. Louise is unfortunately not here at the moment…"

I look at him in surprise. I didn't know that Louise was married. "We've been busy getting ready," he says.

"Is there anything I can help with?" I ask.

"No," he says. "I was just thinking…would you mind waiting in the library till Louise comes back?"

"No." When he begins to walk, I can see that he limps, and that one of his legs is longer than the other. He goes ahead, out into the entryway and continues up the stairs to the first classroom. He opens the door to a brightly lit, dusty room where there are shelves, stacked with books, along all walls.

"You've read something about European mysticism, haven't you?" he asks and limps to one of the bookshelves.

"No."

He briefly looks at me, surprised, and pulls a leather-bound book from the shelf. "Then you should read this book. The author is one of the few western philosophers who have managed to recognize what we call reality." He hands me the book, and I look down at the outside cover with its gold-engraved pattern. "He proves the reality is found here," he says and touches his forehead with a finger. He is looking down at the floor, and it seems like he is falling into a profound contemplation of this.

I look at him with curiosity, waiting for him to explain what he said, but it appears as though he has sunk into his earlier state of absence. Then something sets him off, and he looks up. "I'll go downstairs," he says. I sit down with the book and hear his steps disappear down the staircase. He seems odd, not like a man I would have imagined Louise being married to.

* * *

It's time for dinner when I enter the dining room. In the course of the afternoon, I heard cars drive into the courtyard at regular intervals, and a soft sound of voices reached me through the window And from the stairwell. In two long lines people are standing next to the chairs at the dinner table. I'm standing in the doorway, uncertainly trying to catch the eye of Louise who is standing at the far end of the table. She gives me a sign to come to her and points to the empty seat by her side.

"It was good that you could come," she says with a smile.

She is wearing a black dress and is barefoot, and she has put up her black, curly hair in a ponytail. After so much time that I haven't seen her, I again get an overwhelming impression of something alive in her appearance. Joakim who stands next to her appears changed. He looks awake and present. Louise turns to the others.

"Welcome," she says, "let's sit down and eat."

I look around at the participants most of whom are middle-aged women with clean, wrinkled faces without make-up. Nearly all of them have hair that is gray or dyed auburn, and wear clothes that look like they made them themselves. I get the impression they are the kind of liberated women Mom would get upset about when she saw them on television. At our table stands an older man with a full beard, at the other table stands a younger man with a slender body and a round babyface. He has round glasses and a little mustache. Other than Joakim and me, these are the only males.

It's quiet in the room, and chairs scratch over the floor as we are taking our seats. Louise nods toward the man with the mustache.

"Would you tell us what your name is?"

"Yes," he says with a surprisingly dark voice. "My name is Anders."

While he is speaking, Louise leans over to me.

"Joakim and I can't leave the table," she whispers, "won't you be so sweet to help us bring the food in?"

The voices of the people who introduce themselves fade out and come back while I'm moving in and out of the kitchen. When I've brought in all the dishes, I sit back down in my spot. I stick the fork into the gray, sticky mass Louise has left on my plate and cautiously taste it.

"God," exclaims a woman whose name I haven't caught, "this tastes almost like chicken. It's been at least four years since I last have tasted that. You wouldn't believe this was millet."

We laugh.

At her side sits a tall, slim woman who sticks out above the others. She has smooth, gray shoulder-length hair and strong, sunburnt skin with a lot of small wrinkles. That must be Susanne who introduced herself by that name. I catch myself the entire time staring over at her. There is a superior self-assurance in the way she moves, with her head held up high and coordinated hand movements. She looks up, catches me watching and smiles. I look away in embarrassment.

* * *

Louise opens the door to a brightly lit room with white walls.

"This is where you'll stay," she says and steps aside.

There are a bed, a folding chair, a small table and a cabinet in the corner.

We are in the wing that leads up to the farmhouse. From the utility room, we walked across the courtyard and through a long, white-walled hallway, and this is the last room.

Louise sits down on the bed and strokes her hand over the carpet. I set down my suitcase and sit on one of the chairs.

"I'd like to say thank you for letting me come," I say.

62

She smiles. "Perhaps you'll help us a bit with the practical stuff."

"Yes," I say, "of course."

"Did you have problems with your parents?" she asks.

I blush a little.

"Just a bit," I say. "It doesn't mean anything."

"I don't understand why you don't move away from home," she says.

I don't know what to answer. Every time I think about that, I get scared at the thought of loneliness. I can imagine how difficult it must be to sit alone in a room in an anonymous town. Mom and Dad also have said they don't believe that I would make it.

"I'd like to wait until I grow a little older," I say.

I'm enjoying the sensation of being surrounded by people and being in Louise's company. I hope she'll be sitting here a bit longer. I look over at her, and, again, I get the feeling that I don't know her. I feel like asking her why she invited me, but I can't get myself to do so.

"Look forward to the start of our meditation," she says. "I'm curious to know what you'll think of that."

"I thought we had already begun that," I say.

"Yes," she says, "but this is something different. What we did in the evening classes wasn't real meditation. This course is for advanced students."

I look at her in surprise. Have I become an advanced student?

She says nothing, and I'm thinking desperately what to talk to her about to get her to stay put.

"I didn't know you were married," I say.

Louise laughs. "I've been married to Joakim for over ten years," she says. "When I met him, I was just beginning to be interested in personal development, but it was him who put it all together for me."

She smiles and leans back.

"It may surprise you to hear that I lived a totally ordinary life before I met him. I was married to a lawyer, and I taught at a school, but I was dissatisfied with my existence. It almost embarrassed me because I had a good enough life, but it was like something was missing, a higher meaning to life. It was as if I was being devoured by gray boredom."

"It was nearly a miracle that I met Joakim. He was finishing up his studies at the university, but he had lost interest in his subject, philosophy. I think it was too theoretical. In some way, it was very romantic. I gave up everything for his sake, and he never finished his studies. Afterwards we found the farm here. It's all about daring to take a chance."

She hesitates. Then she says, "It's him who has taught me all I know. Have you noticed that he is limping?"

I'm surprised at her forthrightness.

"Yes," I say.

"He was in a terrible car collision shortly after we'd moved here. For a long time, I didn't know if he would survive. The doctors had to remove several centimeters of his thighbone."

She looks at me with a smile.

"I think we can help you," she says. "I think you need some self-confidence."

She gets up.

"Sleep well. I'd better get on my way back."

In the door, she turns.

"See you tomorrow, early. We start at six o'clock."

I stay where I am and look around in the room. I can hear soft sounds from nearby rooms, voices talking, doors opening and closing. I'm still having a hard time understanding how lucky I've been. It's strange to think that only a day has passed since I was lying on the beach, not knowing what to do with myself.

Through the large window in the gable, we have a view over a meadow with high grass where three horses are moving about and some birds are chasing insects in the air. We are in the farthest wing, in a high-ceilinged rehearsal hall. Across from me, there is Susanne and to my side a tall, strong woman whose name is Else. We've only just got started because there was a line of women waiting in front of the toilet this morning. In the last hour that we've been here, cars have stopped several times out on the courtyard with people headed for the beach, and their faces have been curiously looking through the window pane to see what we were up to.

We must make quite a strange sight. Louise has asked us to stand with our legs spread, our knees slightly bent and hips pushed forward. Our arms are at chest level and nearly stretched out into the air. "Find the spot where it feels as if your arms are floating on their own accord, on a cushion of energy," says Louise while she is walking in and out among us straightening out our body positions.

That's easier said than done. My hands feel like dumbbells, and my muscles are hurting from having to resist gravity. As the minutes go by, my arms and legs, like those of the others, start trembling with the effort of maintaining our position. Afterwards, my legs are shaking so much that it must look like I'm involved in an extremely distinctive dance. Louise stops between my stretched arms and critically looks at my body, her head at an angle. She takes hold of my arms and straightens them and pushes my hips forward. "So," she says, "all the tensions come out this way."

I clench my teeth in pain and try to smile. One of the women sits down on the floor with a bump. "I can't do this anymore."

"Good, let's stop," says Louise, "we're getting together in small groups."

"Pooh, I feel beaten," says one of the women.

"Yes, it's hard, but it's been a long time since I felt so at peace with myself," says another woman.

People are slowly beginning to move toward the door. I follow them out to the courtyard where the air rising from the hot paving stones causes the air to flicker. In a corner between two walls, the tall, strong woman, Else, is sitting with a stack of books by her side. She has a round face with bright, smooth hair, and she is wearing a red sweatsuit with a white zipper and white stripes on the sleeves and legs. She looks up and smiles, and the harsh sunlight is reflected in the thick lenses of her glasses. "What sign of the zodiac were you born in?" she asks and opens the book next to her. "No, don't tell me, let me guess."

"Are you interested in astrology?" I ask.

"Yes. At what time were you born?"

"At dawn," I say and sit down and carefully take one of the books, "at the hour of the wolf."

"The hour of the wolf?"

"Yes, the hour when most children are born and when most people die. I would almost have died when I was born."

"Uh—do you think that's so bad?"

"I hate myself. When I see my face in the mirror, I feel like smashing it to pieces. I would like to be someone else." I fall silent and skip over toward Else who is watching me through her glasses. I regret what I said. Fortunately, it doesn't look like she thinks I'm weird or ridiculous.

"Is that the reason you're taking this course?" she asks.

"No…yes…it was Louise who called and invited me," I say. I put the book back and look at her. "Why did you come?"

"Oh. I'm one of those housewives who feel they're stuck. I have two children, a boy and a girl, and even though they mean the world to me, I find it uninspiring to go home. It feels like my whole life is spent on looking after them and on cleaning up. At times, I had the feeling our house was like a box that grew smaller and smaller. I was feeling nauseated. And so I'm coming here because I like Louise." She is silent and looks out over the lawn.

I get the sense that there's something she won't say. I look at my watch. I'm struck by how long I've been talking with a person I didn't even know, and I'm getting up. "I have to help Louise," I say. "I must go."

"Yes," says Louise and smiles, "but I haven't managed to find out what your sign of the zodiac is."

I can't make myself tell her that I don't believe in astrology. "I don't know," I say with a smile and take a step back.

"Then I will tell you when I figure it out," she says with a serious expression on her face.

* * *

It's early in the afternoon and we are on our way to the beach. On both sides of the dusty walkway there are light green salt meadows that give out a mild salty odor. Several peewits run between the lawns, and above us two larks take turns staying motionless in the air. Purple tar cloves and yellow honeysuckle with their strong aroma grow by the wayside. It's the first time that I have the opportunity to look at the environment of the farm more closely.

At the foot of the first range of dunes, we sit down in a large circle by a patch of horsetail. I've never been among so many really different people, and have a kind of feeling of being in a cabinet of curiosities. From where I'm sitting, I have a view of the sea which laps restlessly up on the beach. With the wind in my face, I'm listening to the conversations of the others. A little distance away there's Susanne talking with Louise, and just below me sits a woman whose name is Britt, and she's chatting with Anders. They're all very friendly, but it doesn't look like we have a lot in common. Most of the participants are old enough to be my parents, and I feel inexperienced and naive compared to them. That means that I don't talk that much with them.

Mostly I listen without saying anything myself. It makes me feel quite the outsider.

Anders' little mustache moves up and down every time he says something. I can't help hearing that they talk about sex.

"I agree with you," says Britt eagerly, "sexuality and religiosity spring from the same primordial power. We have to master our sexual powers to stay in our lane. I'm convinced that it is necessary to live a celibate life."

"Yes," says Anders. "I'm usually abstinent, but one day each year I make a big break, pigging out with booze and women."

I squint curiously at him. I have a hard time imagining him in that situation. I don't exactly know how to explain it, but it's like there is something unerotic about him, something I've perceived about many of the others in the days we've been here.

I lean forward.

"I don't understand what religion has to do with sex," I say and blush, because I don't know if I've been just asked a stupid question.

"It's really pretty obvious," says Britt. "Think of all the rituals they have in common. Or think of all the saints from earlier times. It was only because they were abstinent that they saw God."

I'm nodding even though I'm not sure I understand, and I'm falling back into my own thoughts. Perhaps there are a lot of them who live celibate lives. Perhaps it's for this reason that I have this impression that some of them don't radiate any sex appeal.

Most of the participants are vegetarians. The most ordinary of them is a group of overweight women who would like to lose weight. Another group that I keep my distance from and who I call religious in my mind, are talking fanatically about cancer being a psychosomatic illness that can be cured by positive thinking. And then there's a group of women who line up every morning in front of the bathroom, carrying litmus paper and a test tube in their hands, which they use to measure the degree of purity of their morning urine to see if their bodies are in a state of equilibrium. The one who stands out the most is Susanne. It seems as though she doesn't really belong here. She's often sarcastic, and there is something extravagant in the way she behaves.

When we've come back to the farm, I walk back by the former warehouse where we are being housed, and I'm sitting down in the high grass, my back against the wall. Far away in the meadow, I can see Joakim as he's riding, bare-chested, on one of the horses. The other two, the mare and the foal, are nearby.

I try to picture what Mom and Dad are doing at this moment. It's strange not to see them every day. I simply can't imagine losing them. The thought makes me a little depressed.

Joakim has bent forward over the neck of the stud and is riding fast in my direction when the stud suddenly moves aside as if he is scared of something. I get up and shade my eyes with my hand. He climbs down from the horse, limps to the barn, and picks up a hoe that was leaning against the wall. Meanwhile the horse has run back to the others. Joakim walks back to the spot and starts swinging the hoe down into the grass. I climb over the fence wire.

"What is it?" I cry when I've almost caught up to him.

"A viper," he says. "It scared the horse."

In the grass, there lies the long, slain body.

I feel nausea coming up in me.

"Is there something wrong?" he asks.

"I have a thing about snakes," I say. "At one time, two boys tried to force me to touch one."

* * *

It upsets me when Joakim kicks the body of the snake. He walks back to the shed to return the hoe, and I'm sitting back down with my back against the wall. I'm more upset about the sight of the snake than I thought I should be. I can vaguely remember what the summer house looked like, and I can also recall that there came a smell of tar from the roof that mixed with the smell of the heather into a strange, memorable and stirring odor. It had been an uncommonly hot day. I have a sense that it's the first thing I can remember.

Inside the little living room there sounds a small chorus of voices out of the open door. One of them is Mom's. The two boys I was sent out to play with are running around in the heath in their black rubber boots out of sight from the living room window. One of them had a large, forked branch in his hand, one they chased vipers with. I was standing in front of the summer house and followed them with my eyes while I was nervous because they were doing something they weren't supposed to. The adults had told them to leave me in peace. Besides I'd also noticed the looks and smiles they exchanged before they ran out into the heath. I really felt like going in and telling the adults what the boys were doing, but they'd left as they'd said, and I couldn't tell on the two.

Suddenly, the two let out a howl and disappeared on the other side of the summer house. I was standing on the tiled walkway, sticking out my neck to catch sight of them, and I didn't realize that they'd come from behind the summer house until one of the two grabbed me from behind and held me tight. In the opening between the two arms of the branch that the other boy held in his hand, there hung a long limp and scaled body, dangling down. He stuck the branch with the viper directly into my face. It was just about to happen that I'd touch it.

I screamed, and Mom and the other woman came over from the door. The boy who'd been holding me let go, the other tossed the branch and the viper into the heath and took to running. Mom got a hold of me and told me to quit my hysterics, while the other woman was yelling angrily after the boys. Although they knew that it wasn't me who'd done anything wrong, I could feel that Mom was nervous and ashamed of me. Once again, I was a burden.

In the small living room, the sun was shining in through the large windows that took up all of one wall. Mom had taken me onto her lap, and I could sense that she was irritated. The heat was so strong and the room so dusty that I had trouble breathing. Suddenly the door clanged shut, and the light draft disappeared. There was a slight rustle as the boys locked the padlock on the outside. We were locked in.

I was trying not to show a reaction. The grownups pretended they hadn't noticed that the door had been locked. Maybe they thought if no one paid attention to the boys, they'd grow tired of bothering us on their own.

The heat was growing more intense, and I began to sweat with anxiety until I felt like my whole body was covered in sweat. It was like time didn't move forward. I was so anxious that I no longer cared about the snake. I wanted out, now, right away.

Outside the summer house, it was like it grew ever more quiet, and I became convinced that the boys had forgotten us and that we were locked in for good. My heart was pounding hard, and I could no longer sit still on Mom's lap. I slid down and ran to the door and tried to push it open. The warm wood didn't yield. I tried to find another way out, but that little summer house consisted of only the living room and the kitchen, and there was only the one door. I went out into the kitchen and laid eyes on the little window. I didn't know if I could get out through it. Anyhow, I climbed up on the kitchen table and took off the clasps. Then I opened the window and started wriggling out on my belly. I had my upper body halfway out and moved down into the heath when someone grabbed my legs and pulled me back. Mom fussed at me nervously and took me back into the living room in her arms.

In the meantime, the other woman had managed to open the door and was standing on the tiled floor, yelling out to the two boys. Mom apologized to her and set me down. I went outside, sweating, to catch a breath of fresh air, and because I didn't dare be inside. But when Mom and the woman went back inside the living room, I discovered the evil expression in the boys' eyes. I could tell that they thought it was my fault they'd been yelled at.

They began walking toward the place where they had killed the viper. I ran back to the living room but stopped when I felt the heat. I understood that the grownups didn't have a clue about the awful thing that had happened. In a weird way, it dawned on me that I was quite alone.

* * *

I'm on my way across the courtyard to help Louise when I pass Else who is sitting, reclined, in the warm corner, her eyes closed.

"Oh, how tired I am," she says and opens her eyes. "I couldn't sleep last night. I don't know why. It was like my mind was in a wild uproar."

"What's wrong?" I ask and sit down.

"I don't know," she says and wrinkles her forehead, "maybe it's because the exercises are too strenuous."

"I also think they're strenuous," I say and stretch my sore muscles.

Since this morning we've been doing exercises for eight hours.

"Is it the first time you've taking a course like this?" I ask.

"No, last year I took one for two weeks, but that was quite different. I certainly didn't care for that one. It was mostly for people who wished to live like monks and nuns, and our guru was a devil."

"What was the matter with him?" I ask.

"Ah, there were a lot of things…"

She makes a face and sighs.

"One day he asked me, for example, to stack some firewood that lay around on the ground in the forest near the house. That was an ordeal I tell you, and when I was done, he came to see if I'd done a decent job."

She falls silent and lets her gaze wander over the lawn.

"He signaled me to tear the whole stack down again."

"Why?" I ask in surprise.

"It was an exercise. The fact that I'd carried out a tough job meant nothing. The point was that I'd obey each one of his orders."

"Didn't you get angry?"

"No."

She smiles hesitantly.

"I've conquered the anger in me."

"I'm not sure I would have felt that way," I say. "I think I would have left right away."

"Well now, that wasn't so easy. I was desperate when I left home. I needed something to believe in. One way or another it felt like this was my last chance, and then you're ready to accept almost anything that comes your way."

She is silent.

"We did other exercises too," she says, "sexual exercises."

"Sexual exercises?"

"Yes. Haven't you heard of those? It…it's a union between the male and the female through the genital organs. It doesn't really have anything to do with sex, but I didn't care for it. They say that it has a religious meaning."

"That sounds weird," I say.

I feel like asking her if she did the exercise with the guru, but I can't quite get myself to do so.

"I hate religion," I say. "I hate what it does to people. I have a grandma who's deeply religious and she still scares my mom. It is as if she has an inexplicable power over her. I hope I'll never be like that. I hope I'll never submit voluntarily to other people—or God."

She purses her lips in a slight smile and looks down at her hands.

"Fortunately, Louise is totally different."

We both sit in silence until I get up. I'm going into the utility room to rinse the beans that are left to germinate in a row of Mason jars.

* * *

71

A little after twelve o'clock, we're having lunch when Louise comes into the dining hall with a happy expression on her face and a small four-sided box in her hand. In recent days, she's been so busy looking after a lot of people that I've barely spoken with her, and I'm surprised that she has time to eat with us.

On my plate sit carrots, raisins, bean sprouts and thick, white, clumped cottage cheese. I've gotten used to eating carrots, raisins, and bean sprouts at most meals, but I can't get myself accustomed to cottage cheese. All the same I eat it because I don't want to stick out from the others.

Louise sits down at an empty seat and opens the box. On a piece of cotton wool, there's a long thin metal chain with a ring at one end and a piece of brass, cone-shaped, at the other.

"What is that?" asks Ellen who's sitting next to her.

"A pendulum."

"A pendulum?"

"Yes, and I'll show you now how it works."

She picks up the pendulum and puts the ring over her middle finger. She rests her arms on her elbows and lifts the pendulum so that it's hanging free in the air. She puts her other hand on the table next to a bowl full of garlic.

"If I want to find out, for example, if garlic is good for my health, I can let the pendulum reveal that," she says. "You can also use it in other ways. I've heard that there are some people who can find out whether people are dead by swinging the pendulum over a photograph of them."

I don't know what to think. When Louise picked up the pendulum from the box, I thought that she was going to make fun of us or that it was a party game she wanted us to take part in. But she has a concentrated look on her face, and it looks like she's taking it seriously. She moves the pendulum over the space between her hand and the bowl.

"What are you doing?" asks Bente.

"I'm allowing the pendulum to receive the rays from the garlic cloves and from my hand…" she says. "If garlic is good for me, the pendulum will swing clockwise in an arc, and if garlic is not good for me, it will swing back and forth in a straight line between the bowl and my hand. As if it wanted to trace a borderline. Now I'm trying to empty my head of all thoughts other than my two messages to the pendulum. I'm trying not to think that I believe garlic is good for me."

She lifts her arm and, for a moment, lets the pendulum hang over the bowl, and then moves it over her hand. Then she takes it back again over the space in between and lets it slow down. As I expected, nothing happens. I'm leaning back. It seems a little ridiculous, like a superstition, like knocking on wood or being fearful at seeing a black cat walk across the street. I can't understand that Louise believes in this kind of thing. Then I see that the pendulum is slowly swinging in an arc. The arc is growing bigger and bigger but suddenly turns off and starts swinging back and forth in a straight line.

"That was weird," says Louise looking slightly confused. "I was convinced that garlic was good for me."

She sticks a finger down among the garlic cloves and moves it around a bit.

"No, wait," she exclaims triumphantly, "look here. There are some parsley stalks at the bottom of the bowl."

She picks up three or four green stalks and again lifts the pendulum. It makes the same little jerk and swings out into a circle with a growing radius.

Louise, looks up and smiles.

"What did I tell you? With one simple experiment I've determined that garlic is good for me and parsley isn't."

"May I try?" asks Bente who is sitting next to Louise.

The pendulum goes from hand to hand, and everyone tries to make it go into swinging motion. For some, it works, but for others, the pendulum just hangs down without giving a swing.

"Not everyone has the gift for that," says Louise.

I'm pretty sure that I won't get the pendulum to swing when it reaches me. I put the ring over my middle finger and the only thing I can feel is the strange weight. The pendulum swings out in a course resembling a figure eight.

"What are you thinking of?" asks Louise.

"Nothing," I say, almost scared.

I look down at my hand and over to the garlic bowl. The pendulum starts drawing a circle in the air.

"Now it behaves normal," says Else.

Louise leans forward and studies my hand. The pendulum is swinging with an ever-greater radius. I'm thinking of a straight line, and it makes it swing back and forth like a pendulum hanging down under a clock.

"Joakim," cries Louise in the direction of the open door, "come out and look."

Joakim comes in from the kitchen, and I try one more time. I manage to make the pendulum swing in various geometric configurations.

"I can see that he's moving his hand," says Susanne.

"No, I'm sure I'm not," I say, surprised at myself.

"Let's watch one more time," says Joakim, "then we can keep our eyes on your hand."

I concentrate again on the movements of the pendulum and get it to swing out.

"As far as I can see," he says, "you don't move your hand."

Louise reaches over the table and takes my hand. She stretches it out and studies it.

"Do you realize that you have a completely symmetrical hand? Your index finger and your ring finger are the same in relation to your middle finger, and your thumb and little finger are also the same length. That suggests a strong psychic equilibrium."

I'm feeling both flattered and embarrassed and take the pendulum off my finger. I look up and discover that all the others are watching us. Susanne who sits at the far end of the table smiles a little.

A little later, as I'm walking through the room, I discover that Louise has left the pendulum on the table. I lean down and look at it searchingly. I still don't really believe that it has supernatural properties, but at the same time I'm pretty sure I didn't move my hand. I have an idea.

I set two chairs side by side. With little difficulty, I get my hand to fit in the space between them so that I can't move it. Then I take an apple from the fruit bowl on the table and put it on one of the seats. I sit down the same way at the table and wait for the pendulum to make a move, but the only thing that happens is that my arm is beginning to fall asleep.

Sometime later, in the hallway, I run into Louise who is dragging some mattresses and blankets and pillows to the exercise hall.

"What?" she asks and lifts her eyebrows in a smile.

I tell her about my failed experiment.

"So that didn't really work," I say.

"I'm not so sure," she says and laughs at the embarrassed expression on my face. "Of course, it's true that your hand was moving, but that doesn't mean you were cheating. The hand has to be free. Otherwise, the unconscious impulses can't steer it."

"Now I don't know what to think," I say hesitantly.

"Do you absolutely have to hold the proof in your hand before you dare trust?" she asks. "You can also turn your argument upside down and say that your lack of trust was the reason that the pendulum didn't budge. The first time it worked, right? You saw that it moved even though you felt that you didn't move your hand. And what about those parsley stalks? I didn't know they were sitting at the bottom of the bowl."

I'm nodding reluctantly.

"I didn't think of that. Somehow, I feel stuck. Maybe it's me who doesn't get it."

Suddenly it is as though her mood shifts, and she smiles at me.

"Would you mind helping me carry the mattresses over to the exercise room? We are going to have a long exercise today, and I think the concrete floor will be too cold to lie on."

* * *

When Louise's hypnotic voice has disappeared, a penis comes out of the darkness, and I see that it squirts semen in a jerky arc. The semen is bright with a weird kind of fire that is both black and white. Then the penis disappears, and a shiny hemisphere rotates out of the dark. At its edge, a scaly tail comes into sight. Two hind legs of an animal that looks like a lizard follow next, and slowly a full-grown crocodile is being born. The crocodile starts swallowing its own tail and then goes on doing the same with its body. From the distance that I look at it, it looks like it forms a circle that's becoming smaller over time. When the crocodile has eaten itself up to the forelegs, animals begin streaming out of its mouth. First come a bunch of frogs, next large turtles. Then a winged lizard and other big lizards whose names I don't know.

In the center of a spiral, there is an eye with a black pupil and a shiny lens. I'm falling full speed toward the pupil which is the entrance to a wavy tube. I'm moving in through the opening and walking down a winding path where the walls look like they consist of thin, nearly translucent skin that is grooved and smooth at the same time. I'm sliding the final part of the way and fall out of a narrow hole. As I turn around, I can see a ring muscle contract. In front of me dangles an intestinal system that looks like what you see in anatomical illustrations.

The picture of a grotesque woman comes into view. She has a high hairdo, big breasts, a narrow waist and wide hips that continue into two fat thighs. In her lower torso is a gate with two doors. Some mechanism causes the doors to spring open, and a powerful stream of semen runs out. When the stream comes to a standstill, a row of men come walking out through the gate, and I begin to laugh a little. One of the men bends over forward and shows his butthole which emits a ray of strong light. He starts shooting with a revolver, and the ray of light disappears, but when he stops shooting, it returns.

Light and darkness are moving through my field of vision, and a large assembly of black-haired people come into sight. They're wearing loincloths and are kneeling with their foreheads against the ground. They're worshipping a tall shiny figure that gradually transforms itself into a sun which is moving in a circle, while flashing light emanates from it. The people lift their arms above their heads and raise and lower their upper bodies in a common rhythm while they're creeping toward the sun. The sun changes into a different shining object that is weaker than the first one. The people are reaching the shiny creature, and it looks like they're about to assault it, but instead they start leaping over its head and crawling in through its spread legs.

Some of the men lift up the figure and carry it in a golden chair to the edge of my field of vision. The strange creature is leaning back in the men's arms and stretching longer and longer while shining with undiminished strength.

I'm standing in a large, pointed tent that's covered with furs and skins. With inexplicable certainty, I know that somewhere in my vicinity a powerful creature is waiting. I look up and can glimpse his hook-nosed, Indian-looking face above me in the smoke-filled air.

The black-haired people are beginning to come in under a fold of the tent, way below the powerful head. I'm waiting for them to carry in the shiny figure in its golden chair, but instead, a dimly shining snake sneaks in under the fold. In the middle of the pack, it opens its mouth and starts to gobble up bundles of snakes.

The snakes are wriggling and turning every which way and slithering among themselves with playful tongues. Then they transform themselves into flowers. In one of the flowers, there's a humming bee that moves its hind end and stinger up and down in a costume formed by petals. Another flower starts sucking invisible matter out of my body. It's as if a stream of particles is running out of me. I can't stop the seepage, and I let myself be carried away without putting up any resistance. I get instantly sapped until the flower stops it.

A drill with five blades is sliding into my field of vision and begins to drill down into a gray mountain. I am following it through a passageway that stands open. At the other end, I'm sliding out and find myself in outer space where single stars are blinking far away. Underneath me there are still rocks, which tells me that any directionality has ceased to exist. My seemingly vertical descent had, in truth, been a horizontal movement to the other side of the mountain.

Up in the sky, an eagle is gliding, legs stretched and claws out. It nosedives and tears something loose from me—I don't know what. I remain standing at the side of the mountain, and I see how the eagle and its mate who has also shown up are flying into the horizon with a boy in their claws, a boy that is me. Since the birds are so far away that I can barely make them out as two dots, I throw myself into the air to fly after them but, simultaneously, I also keep standing back on the rock.

A frog arrives, swimming in the water at the foot of the mountain. Its skin is a pale white, and I shiver slightly because it makes me think of a full-term fetus. Behind the frog there's a wave of foam, and in a flash a slim white body that is swimming through the water comes into sight. It looks like the frog is fleeing from a snake and fighting for its life. The frog makes it into the gap and is climbing, with an effort, over the sharp angular rocks. It jumps up toward the top of the mountain, where, to my surprise, I lay eyes on a man swinging with a circle.

I throw myself through the circle with a big jump and find myself in outer space. I'm passing by a planet that looks like Saturn but is surrounded by four rings. I'm moving ahead through big and small planets and reach a black, curved wall. I turn around and gasp for breath. Before me lies the whole universe in the cavity of a globe.

Some shots ring out and a row of holes forming a circle appear on the inner surface of the globe. When the shooting stops, the plates that have come loose are concealed inside. A thistle-like plant with long tinted stems on which flowers grow in a strong violet color squeezes itself in through the hole. I'm getting a strong, anxiety-laden sensation that some violent, chaotic powers that rule beyond the boundaries of the universe are breaking into me. I am feeling that a disaster is going to happen, that the world will collapse, and I'm struggling with a desperate feeling that out through the hole I'll meet the powers on their own territory. Outside it's night and the only thing I can see is the flying thistle, glowing with a phosphorescent green color. An icy wind blows through me.

I'm so fearful that I have to open my eyes. My heart is pounding hard, and I'm out of breath.

I sit up. Louise and the others are lying are lying quiet and deep-breathing around me on their mattresses with blankets pulled up over them.

* * *

A little later, as I step into the narrow white room where Joakim has his office, I'm still nervous. I hold my notebook in my hand.

Joakim looks up. On the desk where he sits lie a lot of index cards.

"I'm sorry to interrupt," I say, "but Louise was busy and asked me to speak to you."

"Have a seat," he says and runs a hand through his long thin hair.

He collects the index cards in apparent random order, I'm cautiously sitting down on the chair. I'd rather not admit that I'm a little afraid of him. Most of the time when he's not riding his horse, he's walking around the farm, appearing distant and unapproachable, and I wonder what he's doing. It doesn't look like he's doing anything practical. The few times when we tried to talk, his seeming repose in himself perplexes me. I would rather have talked with Louise, but I have the feeling that I need to talk to someone.

"What was it you wanted to talk to Louise about?" he asks.

"It's those meditations I have. I can't understand what happens in them. The one I had today was very overwhelming. Should I try to read it out to you?"

He nods, and I open my notebook. He is listening to me without moving or saying anything.

"I don't understand why almost always there are snakes showing up," I say and close the notebook, "it's been this way for a long time. It scares me."

I laugh nervously.

"I can't even make myself touch a photo with a snake in it."

Joakim leans forward and sets his elbows on the table. He puts his chin in his hand.

"For how long have you been meditating?"

"We started last winter," I say.

"Why are you afraid of snakes?"

"That I don't know."

"I'm thinking of my experience with the boys in the vacation home, but I don't think it has anything to do with this."

"Snakes are deadly dangerous…"

"Why?"

"They move as fast as lightning, faster than humans," I say, "and their poison is deadly."

He's leaning back again.

"If you're afraid of snakes, you'll have to seek them out. You have to confront yourself with your fear. There is your energy, there are your powers that are bound up in it."

We are both silent.

"At which point during your meditation was the feeling you had most intense?"

"It was very disturbing to penetrate through the universe…" I say, "it was…it was as if I was being invaded."

"When did you feel you were closest to something meaningful?"

I'm thinking about it.

"That was when I was standing in front of the god in the tent. There was something strange about that glowing figure."

"What do you think it means?"

"I don't know."

"Try to think with your emotions. You'll never reason yourself to the answer. Who do you think that glowing figure is?"

I don't know what to reply.

Joakim repeats the sentence again and again in a toneless, monotonous voice. It is as if the sound is standing still in the air between us until the words start vibrating on their own.

"Who do you think it is?"

"I don't know. It…"

Joakim leans back and looks down at my hand. I look down and discover that I've made a fist with my index finger stuck out.

"Who do you think that glowing figure is?" he asks again, and my hand and my finger turn, on their own accord, to point at my chest.

"No," I say and stiffen.

"Yes," he says, "you're holding the proof in your hand. If you feel it, it's correct. Your intuition won't let you down."

I look down at my hand again. I have a sense that his words are pushing me backward up into a corner of the office. It can't be right. My heart is beating hard.

I look up at him.

"But what does it mean?"

"I think it's obvious," he says, "it means that you must keep meditating."

* * *

"May I come in?" asks Else in a loud, nervous voice and nearly pushes open the door to my room.

I think I'd just fallen asleep when I'm woken up by a hard knock on the door. I get up out of my bed, dazed, and blink at the light.

"Yes, of course," I say and step back in surprise.

She's in her nightgown and stares at me wide-eyed from behind the thick lenses of her glasses. Her hair is disheveled, and her eyes are bloodshot.

"I can't stand it anymore," she says.

She sits down but jumps up again and starts pacing back and forth across the floor.

"I'm beside myself," she exclaims in a shrill voice. "I haven't closed an eye all night. These last few nights I haven't been able to sleep. I see visions and my whole body trembles. I think I'm losing it."

"My God, what's happened?"

Instead of a reply, she grabs hold of my arm and shakes it. She seems shut up in herself as if she hasn't heard what I said.

"I don't know if I should go home. If I stay here much longer, I think I'll end up committing suicide. What am I to do?" she yells into my face.

I look at her in bewilderment.

"Don't you think you should talk with Louise?"

I don't know what to do.

"I want to do that too," she says. "I'm just so confused. I don't want to go up to the farmhouse and stir her up at this time. I know well that it sounds completely crazy for my age that I'm afraid to walk out into the dark and up to the farmhouse. I came to think of you. You must excuse me for disturbing you."

"That doesn't matter," I say.

"I just have these awful visions."

"What are they?"

"I have this sensation of being dissolved by…by…"

I'm waiting for her to explain what it is she sees, but she falls silent and looks fearful.

"Should I walk up to the farmhouse with you?"

"Would you? I'm sorry I'm such a burden."

I'm getting quickly into my clothes while Else is sitting hunched over on my one chair, rocking back and forth. She still appears distracted and moans several times.

"Let's go," I say.

It's an unusually dark summer night, but fortunately there's a light on in a window on the first floor where Louise and Joakim have their bedroom.

I knock, and after we've waited a few minutes, Louise opens the door. She looks at us in surprise.

"It's only five o'clock," she says.

"Else isn't doing so well," I say.

I'm staying in the kitchen while Else and Louise go into the dining room. I have the feeling I'd better wait for Else so that she won't have to walk back alone through the darkness. Because it's five o'clock as Louise said, and as the clock in the kitchen shows, it makes no sense to go back to bed. I decide that I may as well begin to prepare breakfast so that it's ready when the others get up in an hour. I don't understand what happened to Else.

While I'm peeling the last carrots, she is running past me. Before I manage to stop her, she has disappeared. The door slams shut, and a cloud of dust rises from the doorframe. I'm putting down the knife and want to run after her, but I stop. Maybe she'd rather be alone.

I pick up a stack of plates and carry it into the dining room. Louise and Joakim are sitting at the one table and talking with each other in low, intense voices. They don't pay attention to me.

"…so many different people," says Louise. "I can't take responsibility for what's going on with each of them."

"No," says Joakim, "we can't start acting as babysitters for Else. It's each person's job to take responsibility for their own life, and, moreover, to…"

I go back to the kitchen. I find it hard to believe that I heard correctly.

A little later, Louise is coming out of the dining room.

"It's nice that you're made breakfast," she says and continues on her way, out the utility door.

* * *

Else has not come in for breakfast.

It's half an hour later, and we're sitting at the breakfast table. It doesn't look like any of the others have noticed that Else isn't here.

"No, she was feeling poorly," says Louise. "I have given her a massage to relax, and she's sleeping now."

"What's wrong with her?"

"She seems to be off-balance," says Louise. "I think she's pushed herself too hard. It happens sometimes that there are people coming to our courses, people who are psychologically unstable. It's a risk we have to run. We can't predict that. As far as I know, she has some personal problems—something to do with her husband. She wouldn't really talk about it, but she obviously blames herself for their relationship being rocky. I understand that last year, too, something went wrong when she was taking a course. Apparently, she and the others were doing sexual exercises with their guru."

"She told me about that," I say.

"Then you may also know that when she came home, she told her husband about that."

"No," I say.

"He forbade her to do the exercises, and he didn't want her to go on any course again, not even this one, even though we don't do those kinds of sexual exercises. I think she feels that she let down her family when she went again."

82

I'm standing at the kitchen table and doing the dishes after breakfast when I make out, through the window, a car driving into the courtyard and parking. A tall man with a full beard is getting out and standing and bracing himself against the farmhouse. A bit later, Else is coming out of the door of the side wing, suitcase in hand. She waves at the man and sets the suitcase down and comes toward the farmhouse at a rapid clip. The door opens, and she steps into the kitchen.

"My husband has come to get me," she says with a thin smile.

She looks better and seems more relaxed.

"You must forgive me for disturbing you last night. I'm feeling quite embarrassed."

"Are you feeling better?"

"Yes," she says. "Louise managed to get me to sleep. I want to go home and try to find myself in peace and quiet. Louise advised that too. But before we take off, I wanted to say goodbye to you."

I'm walking out with her to the courtyard and I'm standing and watching as the car disappears up along the narrow way between the slopes.

The course continues with daily exercises of six to eight hours, and every night we return to our rooms with sore and stiff muscles. I've barely noticed how the days have gone by, and it hits me out of the blue that the course is going to be over. I'm feeling uncomfortable at the thought of having to go back home.

The evening before we must leave, I'm walking restlessly around in the hallways. Nothing like an actual concluding event is being held because most are too tired or in their rooms, but I can't settle down. It must be the thought that I'll have to go home. Outside the air is very heavy. The door to Susanne's room is open and when I walk by, she calls out, "Do you have a moment?"

I stop and go back. She's sitting at her table writing a postcard. She puts down the pen and turns the card upside down.

"I think that you're doing something all the time," she says and takes off her glasses and puts them next to her pen.

"Well, I'm not paying for staying here like you are," I say.

"Can't you sit down and relax for a moment? Wouldn't you like a glass of brandy?"

I'm surprised that she asks, and at the same time I look a little doubtful at her. I'd like to say yes, but I'm not sure that Louise would approve.

"Don't you think that's unwise? I'd say alcohol is not exactly healthy for the body," I say.

"Are you sure you wouldn't like a glass?" she asks and looks at me intently.

I hesitate. "Yes, thanks," I say.

She lights a cigarette and pinches her eyes shut because of the smoke while she's taking a bottle out of her suitcase.

"Do you think we'll have a thunderstorm?" she asks, pouring the brandy into two tooth glasses. "The air is uncommonly heavy."

"It looks that way," I say.

"There you go," she says and pushes one glass over to me.

She nips at the brandy and leans back while she is stretching her arms out over her head. She sighs:

"I really don't know if I can stand going to the exercises tomorrow. I need a day to rest before I have to go home and start working. Besides, I can't stand hearing Britt and Anders discuss cosmic orgasms. What an expression! Some of them are just a bit too far out. If it weren't for Louise…"

"I think you should come tomorrow," I say and look down at the table surface. "It's the daily exercises that get you results, even if you don't feel like it every day."

Suddenly, I can hear how holier-than-thou I sound. It occurs to me that I say something Louise could have said.

Susanne smiles slightly and shoots me a crooked glance.

"I must admit that I've never met as restrained a young man as you. Isn't it a little depressing to be constantly in the company of a bunch of old broads like us?"

"What do you mean?" I ask evasively.

"When I was your age, I was busy getting out into the world, making trouble, getting some experiences. I think you're too young to lock yourself up in this place."

I shove my foot nervously across the floor and don't know what to answer.

"Perhaps," I say awkwardly, "I don't think I care for those experiences…"

I hurriedly drink up, and, when my glass is empty, I get up.

"Thank you," I say and look at Susanne.

She is looking back at me with an ambiguous smile that's both kind and mocking.

The air is still oppressive, and I'm in a bad mood as I walk toward the farmhouse and let myself in through the utility door. From the dining room, I can just barely hear Louise and Joakim talking in the hall upstairs. I sit down at one of the tables. It is as if everything is coming back, the loneliness, the arguments with Mom and Dad, the uncertainties about my future which I have to decide. I'm beginning to feel sick with tension.

I try to imagine what it would be like to keep living here. I'm sure Louise, and sure Joakim, too, wouldn't object. I'm nervously tapping my fingers on the table, and I'm coming to think that I should have told Susanne that I don't care for other people, that I hate them.

I get up and, when I have turned off the lights everywhere, I go back to my room to sleep.

* * *

"Here we are," says Louise.

We're standing in the courtyard, watching cars drive off in a long line. Since this morning the sky has been covered in dark, threatening clouds.

Louise and Joakim turn and start walking back in the direction of the farmhouse.

We get going on cleaning up after the course participants. I woke up with a headache at the thought of having to go home, and I'm feeling oddly fit, like I'm levitating, and both a little too overwrought and a little too worried. I drag sheets and duvet covers out into the hallway where I'm stacking them up high, and while I'm on my knees, scrubbing the floor tiles in the hallway, I can hear Louise rattle around in the rooms. It smells strongly of cleaning fluids, and that odor, combined with the heavy air of pending thunderstorms, makes me feel sick to my stomach. I stand up and go to the bathroom, but when I return I still feel nauseated. I'm in a strange, nervous state of mind, and I'm working hard on making a feeling of manic breathlessness go away. Instead, the feeling grows stronger throughout the day. It's as if my fingers are numb, and I feel a tingling in them.

In the afternoon, I follow Louise to her old, trashy car.

"You're unusually quiet," she says after we've driven a bit, "is it the weather?"

She leans forward and looks through the windshield at the sky. "I bet we'll have a thunderstorm."

"I don't think it's that."

The wind has died down. Out over the fields several large, heavy gray clouds are hanging in the sky.

"Have you heard from Else?" I ask.

"No."

Louise is looking at me searchingly.

"No. Something is wrong. Are you getting carsick? The air is so oppressive. Should I roll down the window?"

"Yes, thank you," I say and run a hand through my hair, "but…I don't think that's the problem. I know it sounds crazy, but…I feel very strange. I've ever been away from home for such a long time. I've been very happy being with you. I almost think that I'm afraid of returning home."

"Is it your parents?"

"I'm not sure," I say.

I can sense that the feeling of isolation and emptiness is becoming stronger the closer we come to the city.

"Tell me honestly," I say and hesitate, "do you think I seem weird?"

"You?" laughs Louise. "No. What gives you that idea? We were happy to have you with us. And even though you have to go home, this is not a goodbye, I tell you."

I lean my head into the neck support and stare through the windshield at the first houses that come into view between the trees. Rain begins to fall heavily on the windshield. I have a feeling that everything is starting all over again.

I'm trying to think what will happen now, but I feel blocked. I should have asked if I could have stayed at the farm. It's too late now.

Through the rain I can see our house come into view.

"Would you let me off here?" I say.

* * *

The front door is unlocked.

"Is anyone here?" I yell as I come into the hallway.

I'm surprised that there's no answer.

86

I go into my room and put down the suitcase. The room looks as I left it. The desk sits by the window, the bed is in the opposite corner and the shelves with my books are along the far wall. It looks like the things have been waiting for me, and that gives me a depressing feeling that everything is the way it used to be. I go back to the hallway and open the doors to the kitchen and to the living room and to all the other rooms, but Mom and Dad aren't anywhere. I have the sensation of walking around in a strange place, and I notice that the empty house is making me nervous. It's like I can't find my way back after having stayed at the farm for so long. I open the door to the basement and call out into the staircase.

"Mom," I call, "Dad, are you there?"

My voice echoes back from the walls, but there's nobody that answers. Though I'm pretty sure they're not in the basement, I walk down the stairs and continue going from room to room. Down here it's just as empty as upstairs.

I'm about to open the door into Dad's workshop, when I think that I hear a soft noise behind me. I jerk my head around. Wasn't there someone who took a step, or was it only my nerves playing tricks on me? Suddenly I get the childish impression that the basement is unnaturally big and desolate. I have a feeling that I'm not alone, and that somebody has noiselessly followed me down the stairs. I'm beginning to think of one of the stories I was reading at the beach. It dealt with a young girl who rushed up and down two winding staircases in a large, deserted office building, fleeing from a mad murderer. I can't remember how the story ended, and my legs are growing weak under me.

I'm standing with my hand on the door handle, but I don't dare open the door for fear of finding myself face to face with a crazed murderer. I try to get control over myself. I'm not a child anymore. It's been more than ten years since it filled me with terror to go down into the basement by myself. The thunderstorm and the gray grooved concrete walls make me think of the Great Flood that I still live in fear of.

Every time there was thunder and the rain fell densely outside the windows, I'd stand on the landing of the stairs and look down on the gray foaming water that rose and rose up from the sewers and ran, first in narrow streams and then in growing lakes out over the basement floor. I'd be standing fearfully staring into the water which didn't seem to have any intention of ceasing to rise. Mom and Dad couldn't drag me away from the stairs. When Dad tried, I hit him and screamed, and once he'd let go of me, I'd run back to the stairwell like drawn by some force of nature. I would be standing there in the flickering light waiting for the rising water to reach me, with an almost old-testamentary premonition that this was the beginning of the Great Flood. It was like the flow of water from a faucet that had gotten stuck. The Great Flood would keep rising and drown the house and the whole world.

A bright light is flashing between the windows and illuminating the walls, and a moment later a bang sounds that is so loud that the windowpanes shake. The thunderstorm must be directly above the house, and, getting fearful that lightning will strike, I quickly walk through the hallway and up the stairs without looking back. I'm getting nauseated again, and it feels as though warm air from an overheated ventilator is blowing by my ankles. I'm going out to the bathroom and looking for a long time down into the white enameled bathtub with that shiny drain. I lie down in it, feeling the cold from the surface come up through my clothes. The thunderstorm is so close now that the thunderclaps follow the lightning almost without an interval. I'm squatting down and turn on the faucet. I put my palm over the hole and feel the suction from the drain and the pressure of the water against the back of my hand as it seeks to stream out. I lift my hand, but it doesn't calm me to watch the water disappear.

Suddenly, I don't understand how other people can believe that water is moving in a never-ending cycle, that it returns to seas and lakes from where it evaporates up into the atmosphere and then again comes down as rain. I have a sense at this moment that all of nature's forces are pulling in the wrong direction.

I get up out of the bathtub. The water is dripping from my shoes and pant legs, but I hardly notice. The twilight in the hallway seems almost tangible as if I can feel it with my fingers. It's like the hallway is divided into zones of warmth and cold. When I've arrived in my room, I push on the light switch. The light doesn't work. Someone must have cut the power so they could hide more easily in the dark. It looks like the shadows glide together to cover a faceless silhouette.

I'm trying to get a grip on myself. Perhaps it's the lightbulb in the ceiling that's busted. I try to light the desk lamp, but it doesn't work either. I'm so fearful that I freeze. I'm listening and waiting for something…someone…to step out of the darkness.

Nothing happens. The fear lets up, and I can move again. I lie down on the bed and listen nervously for the slightest sign of a noise. Only if I'm lying completely still and hardly breathe can I manage to hold out until Mom or Dad comes home, the way I did when I was little and lying alone in my room at night with the blanket pulled up over my eyes to hide from the ghosts. I have an idea and lift my head. Maybe the lightbulbs have come loose. I feel relieved. Of course, that's it. Then it dawns on me that that means that somebody who's still in the house must have unscrewed them, and I fall back onto my bed in fear.

A thunderclap wakes me up. The cold white flash from lightning lights up the room, and I look up into two eyes that gaze down on me. "I didn't know you'd come home." It takes a moment before I recognize Dad's face and the sound of his voice. I sit up and shake my head. "Where have you guys been?"

He looks at me in surprise. He's wearing a black raincoat and his gray hair is wet. "I've been at work as you can figure I suppose. Mom has surely stayed at the office. You know that she doesn't care to be home alone during a thunderstorm. Tell me, is the power out? All circuit breakers are out. And why was the water running in the bathtub?"

"I guess I forgot to turn off the faucet," I say weakly. "Are the circuit breakers out? I thought that someone had cut the power."

"Why did you think that?" he asks and looks at me inquisitively. "You know, don't you, that we wouldn't do that." He straightens up and walks over to the dark window and looks out at the sky. "Have you had a good summer?" he asks. In the semidarkness, only his outline is visible. It sounds as if his voice comes from somewhere else.

"It was terrific," I say and mess up my hair in confusion. I don't know what to tell him.

He turns around and walks away from the window. He is going to the spot where the voice comes from, and stops. "When did you arrive home?" It sounds like his voice is coming over from the window.

"An hour ago," I say and make an effort to keep my mind clear.

Dad puts his hand on the door handle. "We couldn't understand why we didn't hear from you."

Part 3

Tok, tok, tok, tok…the dry branch with the yellow shriveled-up leaf keeps beating against the window with a hard, annoying sound. It's like someone is knocking and wants to come in.

Since coming back from the course in the summer, I've been feeling strange. Other than Mom and Dad, I haven't been with any other people, and our daily exchange of practical, meaningless remarks gives me a deeper sense of loneliness than I've known before.

"Are you finishing up any time soon?" yells Mom and pounds on the wall. "It's been over half an hour since you went into the bathroom!"

"Yes," I call and put the book I'm reading on the sink.

I reach my hand out for the toilet paper and notice that the nausea I've had in the last days is returning. Since day before yesterday my stomach has begun to contract in cramps, causing me to have to go to the bathroom every two or three hours. My hands are becoming red and raw and have started to crack because I wash them so often. It makes me think of the time when I had an irresistible need to wash my hands because I was afraid of spittle and bacteria.

I haven't gone out to visit Louise and Joakim. Since I came back, I haven't been able to see any purpose in anything at all. I haven't been able, either, to pull myself together to make some decisions about my future. The only thing I make myself do is to read and to do my exercises, and I've begun to stay awake until late into the night after having done nothing else all day. It feels different from my earlier indecisiveness, and it seems sick to me that I'm so apathetic. Mom and Dad have apparently given up on me. They no longer talk about what I should do.

The branch hits the window again, and it makes me twitch. It sounds like bones, a skeletal hand, as if a dead person wants to come in.

I have a bad taste in my mouth, and I'm feeling nervous. The nausea rises up in my throat all the time. I'm in doubt about everything. Maybe I can't change at all as I think, maybe I have instead taken the first step through the door into a rubber cell. I'm shivering and have to force myself not to think the thought through to the end. I don't understand where I get those morbid ideas from.

"Haven't you finished yet?" yells Mom and, again, pounds on the wall.

I get up. When I've flushed and washed my hands, I go out into my room, lie down on my bed and continue reading. Then I close the book and lift my head. I have goosebumps and a vague feeling that nothing is real any longer. From a weird, distorted perspective, the walls are leaning in over me and the furniture is coming closer, but without moving. It feels like my hands and my head are swelling. There starts to be a pounding in my temples, and a pressure from inside is pushing them outward. Next the walls straighten up and step out to the opposite side. The furniture is moving away, but, at the same time, I have the sensation that it is me, who's lying on the bed, who's moving— without moving at all.

I'm shaking my head and get up abruptly. My legs are giving in under me and I'm swaying a bit, like a drunk. I don't understand what's happening. I unlock the door and start walking restlessly around in the house, while supporting myself against the wall or holding on to a chair, a table or a door. It seems like the support is not firm. A faint shiver is going through my hands. That gives me a sensation that dead things have become alive.

Mom is sitting in the light at the kitchen table and is darning a pair of Dad's socks. She looks up, a black thread in her mouth.

"Why are you walking around like this?"

"I don't know," I say and carefully let go of the door. I'm leaning on the air to see if I can stand without support.

"I simply couldn't sit still."

"Is it any wonder?" she says and follows me round the kitchen with that dark, accusatory expression she's been following me around with ever since I came back from the course.

The time is after three. I'm lying nervously on my bed, listening to strange noises in the dark. The yellow luminescent numbers on the alarm clock are moving slowly.

There's something that weighs on my nerves. I don't understand what it is, but I'm becoming more and more nervous. I close my eyes and feel a twitch in my body and get the sensation of rising up and levitating above my bed. A strange, big panorama in strong, shiny colors is sliding before my gaze. Even though I'm trying to pinch my eyes more firmly shut, the picture won't go away. I must follow into the glimmering landscape of yellow, red and blue colors that are shining phosphorescently. It feels like I'm falling backward through the air but without hitting the bed. I don't know what I'm afraid of, but I'm gasping for breath like in great danger.

Suddenly, the shiny leaf turns into an axe in the dazzling light. The axe begins to cut the necks of some women on their knees, who are waiting in a seemingly endless line, their heads on blocks. I'm striking out with my arms like someone who's drowning, and I'm sitting up. It looks as though the blood runs in red stripes through the darkness. I'm reaching out one of my arms and turn on the light, but my heart is pounding with fear.

I'm making an effort to calm down for over a quarter of an hour, trying to soothe myself so that I should be able to sleep when I lie down. The moment I switch off the light, the figures again come out of the darkness even though I haven't closed my eyes. It is as if the night is filled with barbarous savagery. Some limits I didn't know have broken down. I have a feeling that the darkness is lying open below me.

The numbers on the clock are moving so slowly that it looks as if they don't move at all. Every time I look at the alarm clock, only a few minutes have passed. I close my eyes again, but all of a sudden, instead of falling asleep, I'm in a terrifying medieval world where men and women are exposed to cruel and barbarous assaults. Men with black hats and bare chests are carrying out brutal acts. I can't stand watching. I don't think I've ever been this fearful.

It's starting to lighten up outside the window, and at the first rattling sounds from the kitchen, I decide to get up. I'm too scared to lie down, and I don't believe I'll be able to sleep. Other times when I suffered from sleeplessness, I would have fallen asleep at this point in time.

Mom is standing over the stove and turns her head when I come in.

"It's really early for you to be up."

"I couldn't sleep."

She keeps looking at me while she's cleaning the stove, but I pretend that I don't notice. There's no reason to tell her that I've been lying awake all night. I'm convinced that tonight I'll be able to fall asleep. I probably wasn't tired enough because I didn't do anything all day. But I don't understand where the scary visions come from. It must be something transient.

I take a plate out of the kitchen cabinet and sit down at the table. At the sight of food, I become nauseated. It's like a hand is twisting my guts, and I get up.

"Just a moment," I say, and as I come out into the hallway, I'm jogging to the bathroom. I rinse and wash my hands. Then, for no reason, my legs start shaking so strongly under me that I have to lean on the sink.

It's early afternoon, and I'm alone in the house. I've sleepily sat down on the floor and pulled my legs up underneath myself. All morning I haven't been able to pull myself together to do anything, and I'm too tired and nervous to lie still and read.

For some reason, it makes me anxious to do my exercises. Each time I bend my arm or stretch my leg, it's like the movement sends energy up into my head, and, instead of calming me down, the exercises make me nervous. My body has become lithe, and I can easily assume any of the positions that I couldn't do before. I'm putting my fingers on the back and along the sides of my nose, and I'm breathing in a slow, deep rhythm to try and settle down. Then I get overwhelmed by sleepiness and lie down on the floor. My eyelids droop, and I'm yawning.

The heaviness I feel comes from something lying in my palm. I'm looking over my chest and catch sight of a carving that represents the face of an angel. The face is yellowed, and the nose is fractured in a crooked, broken angle. It must be carved in ivory. By my side in the burial vault, there's an open casket, and I cautiously lay my head down on a white pillow. The lid of the casket, which stands up against the damp, sodden wall, is made of fine carved wood and has a small square window in its broad upper half. I lift the lid and place it over the casket. It slips out of my hands and falls in place with a loud noise as if someone from inside pulls it down. I'm leaning over the casket, looking at the angel's face through the square window. It stares back at me with live eyes, and the corners of its mouth open and reveal two fangs.

It's me that's lying in that close darkness, staring out at the world through the square opening that's covered by glass while I'm blinking furiously with my eyelids. I see everything, nothing human can stay hidden from me. I am penetrating it with my eyesight.

In a room, an old sick man with white hair and a wrinkled face is lying on a bed. Another man with a black cloak on his shoulders is standing bowed over him. The man raises his arms so that his cloak unfolds and leans in over the sick person. He lets his gaze run along his neck where a vein is pulsating restlessly. He smiles and bares two fangs. Then he slowly leans still farther forward and puts his mouth to the sick man's ear.

"Calm down," he whispers while saliva is running down his chin. "I've come to help you."

The one on the bed stretches out one of his arms and points a trembling finger at an empty bed.

"My son, they've taken him."

He lets his arm sink and moans weakly, "Let's pray for his soul."

The standing man takes a step backward and turns around. He bends forward and looks like a bat, in that he's running, with his cloak spread out, toward an open hatch through which he disappears.

In the burial vault underground, he hurries toward the casket where I'm lying and looks at me through the window glass. The lid is being lifted and set against the sodden wall. He lets his index finger slide down over the stones and turns to me.

"Child of my blood," he says and draws a black halo of soot on the white cover I'm lying on all around my head.

A sudden feeling of horror wakes me up, and it twitches in my body as I'm coming to. I'm about to get up from the floor when I get the sensation that a salivating mouth with two fangs is biting down on my neck. Instinctively I put both my hands over my carotid arteries to protect them. Then I put my hands down. What is going on?

It's been a long time since it got dark. I've been walking restlessly and uneasily all over the house, while trying not to think of the vampire. But the discomfiting thoughts keep bearing down on me, and I can't stand being alone with them. I open the door to the living room where the blue light from the TV is lying like a deep, secretive glow on the furniture. Mom and Dad are sitting with a table between them and watching a nature film. On the table are coffee cups, a plate with cakes, and a thermos. Mom is knitting a cardigan while she's following the movie.

"Can we play cards?" I ask, standing by Dad's chair.

He looks at me probingly. Then he nods.

I'm trying to keep up a strained conversation while we're playing. I can't remember ever trying to talk with him without a specific purpose, and it is almost terrifying to discover that we have nothing, absolutely nothing, to talk about with each other. I'm so tired that I could fall asleep on my chair, but I don't dare to turn in and try to sleep. What if I can't? I look at my watch. It's been thirty-six hours since I last slept.

A bit later, the clock strikes eleven.

"This will be our last game," says Dad. "I'm tired and I'll have to be up early."

He deals the cards.

For a moment, I consider telling him how anxious I am. I almost wish he could sit by my bedside until I've fallen asleep. But I can't get out the words. I've begun to form a suspicion that it's due to the meditations that I can't sleep. I don't understand but is as though they've hidden in place before sleep, and they block it. If I tell him, he'll either not understand, or he'll for sure blame me that I've brought this on myself. I'll have to make it on my own. There may not be any reason to tell. I may be able to fall asleep without any problem.

Dad is getting up.

"Goodnight," he says, "sleep well."

"Yes, you too," I say and yawn.

I'm waiting nervously until Mom and Dad have finished in the bathroom. When I come into my room, I'm slowly taking my clothes off and crawl in under the blanket. I don't know yet if the visions will come again, but I'm nearly certain they will. It's quiet in the house, and the only sound I can hear is the pounding of my heart, uneasy and fast. I cautiously close my eyes, lying in the comfortable darkness without visions. I'm so tired that, to my relief, I'm beginning to feel that I'm about to fall asleep, when, all of a sudden, my body starts shaking, and the first landscapes appear out of nothing to my closed eyes. I'm sliding at great speed down a black tunnel that ends in a luminous grotto where sweating, half-naked men of the Inquisition are waiting for me to start their massacre. My field of vision becomes colored red, and blood is flowing everywhere. I'm moving, unable to prevent it, from one grotto to the next, and I'm forced to watch all conceivable kinds of cruelty. Women who are being raped and slaughtered by men with axes. Death-bound convicts who are beheaded on the scaffold. Torture…

I can't bear looking at this. I'm so scared as if it was I, myself, who was standing in front of the executioners, and I let out a gasp and open my eyes wide. I turn on the light and, just like the night before, sit at the headboard of my bed, while my teeth are chattering with an idiotic clattering sound. It feels like being punished, but I don't know what I've done. I don't think any longer that I'll be able to sleep. I get up and take a book from the shelf, and while the night is passing, I slowly turn the pages without being quite clear on what I'm reading.

It's early in the morning, and my eyes are so tired that I barely can make out the letters. I yawn and my eyelids keep closing. I'm lying down, desperate to try and sleep, but as soon as I close my eyes, the unbearable visions show up again, and I wake up. It's like I have a poison in my body. I don't dare to take sleeping pills because I know that their effect will make me so nervous that it will be still harder for me to fall asleep. Since I threw out the pills when I was eleven and couldn't swallow my spit, I've avoided taking pills.

I yawn and get out of bed. I'm so tired that I have headaches, and while I'm getting dressed, the nausea returns, and I have to run out to the bathroom so as not to poop in my pants. I'm sitting on the seat, and while my stomach contracts and empties, things around me start changing their appearance. Out of the corners of my eyes I can see shadows and weak hints of movements, but no matter how quickly I turn my head, I can't do it fast enough to manage to see them. I know very well that they're not there, but I keep seeing them.

* * *

The weather is cold today, almost like winter. I'm standing on the tiles in front of the house, and I discover that I can now also see the visions with my inner eye, when I stare up into the sun and let myself get blinded. It's been three nights since I slept, and I need to ask somebody for help. This night went just like the two preceding it, but I notice that the intensity of the visions has grown stronger. I don't dare to lie down to sleep anymore. My bed has turned into a hostile place.

I'm driving the car out of the garage and turning onto the way to the farm. For one reason or another, it's like the car has a will of its own and wants to stray over the roadside all the time. My hands begin to tremble so strongly on the steering wheel that I have to stop. When they seem to be calm again, I slowly drive on, by fields lying fallow. The earth is black and thick with wetness and gives me a sense that it is here, in the tree-lined squares, that the night keeps itself hidden while it's day. The trees are like trolls in boxes which jump up from the roadside to make my tired eyes sting with pain.

I blink and turn into the gravel road, and as I'm doing so, I get the sensation of being pursued. In the rearview mirror, I perceive a subtle change in the landscape, but when I look back, there's nothing unusual to see. I feel a stinging in my head from anxiety, and I get the feeling that a stranger is sitting in the rear seat. I automatically put my hand on my pulse: It's pounding nervously. Then, in a dangerous movement, I turn my head back, because I have the feeling that the vampire is sitting in the seat behind me. Although I step on the accelerator, I can't get away. Even so, my foot imperceptibly comes to press the accelerator down more and more, and I'm driving faster and faster over the pothole-covered road while I'm breathing heavily with fear, and cold sweat is breaking out from my palms.

The farm comes into view under the slopes, and I slow down. I drive slowly into the courtyard and park. For some reason, I'm feeling a strong, inexplicable reluctance to walk toward the farmhouse. I can see myself walking around between the buildings, but I can't recognize myself. It is as though it is a different person. But I know no one other than Joakim and Louise whom I can ask for help, and I have to talk to somebody. I'm hoping that Louise is home, for I don't care for the idea of talking with Joakim.

I get out of the car and walk uncertainly up to the farmhouse door, and I knock. After a moment the door is opened, and Joakim is standing in front of me. For that brief moment as we are facing each other in silence, it is as if I'm fumbling my way through a dark room to find the switch and turn on the light so that I can see which ghosts I'm in the room with. Perhaps it's me who has never been able to tell dream from reality. With a chill, I reject that thought.

"Is that you?" says Joakim in surprise, and I think I can hear a strange, dismissive tone in his voice.

He is, as usual, in his checkered shirt and blue, well-worn jeans.

Then he says, "We'd nearly given up on ever seeing you again."

"There's something wrong," I exclaim, "I'm anxious. I can't sleep. I haven't slept in three nights."

"Come on in."

He takes a step back.

"Louise isn't home," he says.

The sound of our steps hits my ears from the stone floor, while we're walking through the hallway, and a pervasive smell of herbs that I haven't noticed before is waving in through my nostrils. I can tell that my senses are more acute than they used to be. We're sitting down in the dining room, and I tell Joakim what's been happening. His facial expression is calm, and somehow, I feel he's not as surprised as I'd expected. My voice cracks several times, and then I'm sitting in silence. To my ears my voice sounds distant, like it's someone else, somewhere else in the room who's speaking.

"It's your ego, your personality that is being broken through by forces," says Joakim, "through the exercises you've opened channels to your unconscious."

"What?" I say.

I haven't heard him talk this way before, and my tired brain has a hard time understanding what he's saying. His play with words annoys me: personality, ego, unconscious, channels. It sounds like building blocks, not like it has anything to do with a human being, with me. I'm yawning loudly and getting tears in my eyes.

"Well, what am I supposed to do?"

"I think you should take it easy and see if you become yourself again in the course of a few days. What will help you the most is sure to be some hard, physical work. You're losing your groundedness."

I'm breathing heavily. It feels like something is stuck in my neck.

"Well, what should I do? I need to get to sleep at night, otherwise I think I'm going nuts."

Joakim looks at me in surprise.

"Fine," he says, "I'll give you an exercise that you should do just before you go to bed. You must go out into the backyard and dig a hole in the ground. Then you have to stand in it, barefoot."

"What?" I say.

I look at him doubtfully.

"Well, will that help?"

"It will ground you."

"How long do I have to stand there? Till I grow roots?"

I let out a weird, hysterical laugh. I don't know what to think. The exercise he proposes seems totally unconnected to what's happening to me.

"You must stand in the hole for five to ten minutes," he says, "until you feel the connection to the earth."

I get up and say goodbye to Joakim and walk out into the twilight. As I'm sitting down in the car, the feeling of being pursued by a stranger returns. I force myself to turn and look carefully down into the space between the seats, but there are no vampires, no murderers, nothing dangerous visible.

* * *

The time is 11:30, and I'm sneaking out of the house. In the garage, I pick up a spade and walk to the farthest end of the backyard, where I'm digging a hole. Some translucent clouds are gliding above my head through the light from the moon. It's cold, and my breath is visible, but the ground is no longer frozen. The sods and the hole in the ground make me think of death. I feel like a gravedigger in a churchyard who's digging his own grave.

The hole looks like it's deep enough, a few more sods, and I pull off my socks, alternately balancing on each leg in one of my shoes. I walk up to the hole barefooted, and for a moment I'm standing on the edge, unable to take the step into the cold, damp darkness. I don't think that the exercise will work. But I've read that at times the most improbable action is the correct one. Sometimes it's just better to do something than not to do anything. I step into the hole. For a long time, I don't notice anything happening, nor do I know what is supposed to happen. For some reason, I imagine that I'll be hit by a blow that nails me to the ground like you ram a pole down. Still nothing is happening. Should I maybe fill the hole with the dirt I've dug up? I stretch out my hand and grab the spade and fill in the dirt around my legs.

My feet are freezing and my teeth are clattering with cold, and I'm beginning to get impatient. I have a feeling that I'm just about to cry. In the weak light, I can make out the hands on my watch. I must have been standing in the hole for more than a quarter of an hour. The exercise isn't working, or else, it works but I haven't found out. Perhaps I will only feel it when I go to bed. Just to be on the safe side, I remain standing in the hole for another five minutes.

I step out of the hole and cover it so Dad won't discover it. Then I put the spade back in its place in the garage and go inside. I'm feeling still more disturbed than I was before. When I've entered my room, I'm lying cautiously down on my bed and close my eyes. I'm more fearful now that Joakim has told me what the matter is, and I can sense that the visions are stronger than before. Maybe I'll never get to sleep again, but every time slip into a state of meditation. I don't know how long a person can live without sleep, and I don't dare think about it. Louise would surely say that it's because I don't believe in the exercise that it doesn't work.

I debate whether I should go in and wake up Mom and Dad, but I can't get myself to do that, so instead I nervously take a book and try to read.

* * *

"Why aren't you eating your food? What's the matter with you?" asks Mom.

"I'm not hungry," I say und look at her with wide open eyes.

I can smell that I emit a weak sour odor. I've stopped bathing and changing clothes. Why should I wash up when my body secretes sweat and smelly liquids regardless? And why should I change clothes when they're dirty after a day and need washing again anyway? It seems stupid, and the thought makes me tired. Dirt comes back no matter what. I don't understand how Mom and Dad haven't noticed the smell.

"You have dark circles under your eyes," she says and looks at me. "Don't you sleep at night?"

I don't dare tell her that I haven't slept for seven nights.

I've never heard of people who haven't slept for such a long time. I'm feeling out of it, and my body hurts from lack of sleep, but I'm making an effort to pretend that there's nothing wrong so that Mom and Dad won't find out what's happening. I don't want them to blame me. During the day I manage to make them believe everything is the way it used to be. I'm pushing the plate away and get up.

I go back into my room and sit down, tired, behind my desk, pretending that I'm reading. My body is stiff, and my nerves feel stretched like strings as if they were what holds me upright. I'm yawning, and I have to hold my eyes open so as not to start seeing the visions in broad daylight.

I get the idea that it could perhaps remove the tension from my nerves if I masturbated. Only half there, I unbutton my pants and play with my penis. But even though I push and pull on it and think of stimulating images, it's staying limp. I button up my pants. It's like I'm done with my bodily functions.

I can see that the weather is clear, but all the same, the road lies under a haze outside the window. I'm slowly drawing my gaze back to me and looking down at my desk. It's as if the chair were pulled out from under me. In the spot where the desk stood a moment earlier, there is a weird gnarled, glistening box that is moving in a slightly pulsating rhythm. The floor has transformed itself into a slimy, metallic-shimmering mass of algae from which a rotten smell rises, like from a sewage tank. The whole room is bent out of shape and is breathing heavily like a large, threatening organism, and an odor of decay and a sensation of horror sweep in over me.

I'm shaking my head to make the frightening nightmare disappear. Then it occurs to me that it may not be a nightmare. Maybe what I see is something others can't see. Maybe it's the way things are before I have perceived them through my senses.

I hide my face in my hands with anxiety.

When I look up, the room and things in it have returned to their normal appearance, but I don't dare to lay my hands on the tabletop or touch the book. I'm also afraid to touch the floor with my feet, but I force myself to stand up.

I'll have to drive out to the farm again.

* * *

It's Louise who opens the door.

"Now you'll have to help me," I exclaim. "I don't dare…"

"Joakim told me that you were out here before," she says and studies my face. "I can see that you're not doing well."

"May I come in?" I ask.

She steps aside, and we go into the kitchen, and I sit down at the table. Louise has made tea, and she is putting two mugs on the table. We're drinking in tense silence.

"You're not doing better then?" she asks and puts her mug aside.

I look at her in surprise. Her voice sounds hard, and I sense a hostile attitude in her, as though she means that it's my fault that I can't sleep.

"The exercise Joakim suggested didn't help?"

"No," I say. "I'm doing rather worse. It's been seven nights since I slept. Everything is becoming more and more weird. I'm so tired, I think I could sleep standing up, but I can't fall asleep. I'm afraid to try. Every time I close my eyes, I get these spooky visions that keep me awake."

"What is it you see?"

"The most awful stuff. Murder, assault, cruel torture. Today it was like my room was dissolving. What am I doing wrong?"

Louise has been sitting with her head bent down, looking down into her mug. I think her eyes are glistening a little when she looks up and meets my gaze.

"What's happened is that you've come in touch with forces in your self, as we call it. You've broken through into…into chaos, into the cosmos, into the divine in yourself. You may better understand it if I say that what you're experiencing now is something I've dreamed of and struggled to experience for many years."

"What?"

I can't believe what I'm hearing. Am I so far gone in my tiredness that I no longer understand what other people are saying?

"Are you saying that you'd like to experience what I'm going through?" I ask hesitantly. "I have to tell you that I have a hard time imagining a divine condition that seems devilish to such a degree."

Louise is smiling.

"That's because you look at the things the wrong way. Your ego is dissolving in order to merge with your self. You're on your way up into a supernatural being where all and nothing are one and the same. That's exactly what we work so hard to achieve. It's another matter that your development has surely been happening far too fast."

"So there may be something I misunderstood," I say harshly, trying to control my voice.

"I thought what we were working toward was an expansion or overcoming of our own limitations, but what's happening now is that I'm about to disappear in a void."

Louise is smiling weakly.

"Is it self-realization you're thinking of? That's what some call it. It's what we used to call it in our evening courses. Actually, it's exactly the opposite we're working toward. Didn't you know that?"

The meaning of her words comes to me with a delay when she has stopped talking. I'm sitting still, letting the words sink in. Suddenly I can imagine the room that was dissolving. My hands begin to shake.

"No," I say, "that wasn't clear to me."

I'm drawing in my breath with a whistling sound.

"Does this mean I'm losing my senses? Does it mean that I'm ending up going deaf, blind and mute? That I'm becoming a mental patient, in a rubber room, or, even worse, a zombie…a zombie," I repeat and hear my voice breaking.

Louise doesn't answer, and I continue anxiously: "It was to come in contact with other people that I started going to your classes." I'm so angry that I start spitting. "Harmonious people with well-functioning lives. Ha. I don't even have a sexual desire any longer. Does that mean being well-functioning? Does that mean saying yes to life?"

Louise stops smiling and leans back in her chair. "Yes, but on a different plan. The sick imaginations are being burned out of your mind. You must learn to understand that life is an illusion."

"Well, I don't wish to see through life," I say and groan, "all I want to do is live it."

"If you try to halt your development, you can sustain damage to your soul. What consequences that has for your next incarnation I won't be able to say."

"My next incarnation…" I say angrily and wipe the spit from the corners of my mouth with the back of my hand, "when have I ever said I believe in reincarnation? And if I did believe in it…how will I be able to think of a coming life? I don't know how I'll continue living this one. I have already sustained damage; I have already become marked. How could I ever forget this week? What should I do to make it stop? How should I fall asleep?"

"If you like," says Louise and hesitates, "I can talk to one of our friends who knows more about this than Joakim and I do. Should I call and ask him what he'd advise you to do?"

I'm nodding slowly. I don't know what else to do. Louise gets up and closes the door to the living room after herself. I'm waiting, riled up, in the stillness while I'm yawning and nervously tapping my fingers on the tabletop. Slowly I'm beginning to calm down, and it feels like I'm being buried in my tiredness.

Louise returns and sits down.

"Sten doesn't have time to take you into treatment at the moment, but he said it would be best if you don't do the exercises for a while."

"I stopped doing the exercises," I say, "and I don't dare to start them up again either. Now I know how that ends."

We're sitting in silence.

"I just don't get it," I say, discouraged. "I've always said that the exercises were the only correct way, but now it suddenly seems like they're the devil's work themselves. Soon I won't know what to think or where to turn. It is as if everything is collapsing right in front of my eyes. Did Sten say what I should do to go to sleep at night?"

"No…" says Louise and hesitates, "but perhaps you can use an exercise that at times I use myself when I can't fall asleep. I'm sure it won't hurt you."

I look at her in resignation. I'm so desperate that I think I'm ready for anything if it can help me go to sleep.

"When you're lying in bed, you'll imagine a dome of glass that stretches over your body from head to foot. Look out through it and try to see God. Then, I promise, you'll fall asleep."

I nod, tired, even though I think it sounds strange.

"Does it help?"

"It used to help me."

"But I don't believe in God."

"That doesn't matter," she says, "try it anyway."

"Am I going insane?"

"No, of course you aren't," she says.

She casts a look at her watch and looks up with a smile.

"Unfortunately, you'll have to go. I don't mean to kick you out, but I have a class that starts in half an hour."

I'm getting up.

"Take it easy," she says, "try to relax. Tonight, you'll be sleeping."

* * *

The night is almost over. I'm up, alone, like it's becoming a habit. I've opened my eyes wide, and I'm staring at the light. The room appears to be humming softly. On the whole, it's getting harder and harder to perceive the earth as a stable, dead mass. It is shifting on the surface and moving where I put my feet. I put my hand in front of my mouth and yawn.

I'm forcing myself to go to bed. I have to do violence to my thoughts to prevent the visions from showing up, and instead, I'm trying, as Louise said, to see a large glass dome over myself. I have a feeling that the dome is becoming gradually more and more visible, until it sits like a gleaming arc over my body. The nightmarish visions are pressing in before my eyes, but I'm pushing them back. Several times it almost looks like distorted faces are pressing in on the glass. I'm slowly getting the sense that I'm lying in a coffin.

I try to conjure up the picture of God. Then I realize that I forgot to ask Louise which god she was thinking of. I'm trying desperately to find an answer, but I can't. I don't want to think of an Indian god. Instead, I center my thoughts on the concept as such.

After a while, it feels as if something is touching me way down at my feet. I direct my attention toward the spot and begin, in my thoughts, to drag the black figure to the top of the dome. A face is slowly rising over the glass arc, like a moon, while the body remains hidden in the darkness. The face descends toward me, in a kind of heavy calm, and in a flash that's both surprising and natural, I recognize God. He looks exactly as I imagined Him when I was little. A big, bushy, white beard, a brown, wrinkled face, and two eyes that are glowing like coal. His face has a strangely mournful expression.

God's face is hanging above me for a long time, like a balloon on a string. It's oddly distant and close at the same time. Suddenly, even though I haven't done anything, the face falls apart and, the next moment, the glass dome bursts with a loud, sharp sound. It's as though the shards are falling clankingly down on me, and I can feel the sharp sting of pieces of glass boring into my skin. I'm lying motionless with pain, and I can feel the tears flowing over my face. The only thing I can see are the contours of an inhumane world.

Soon after, the first daylight comes in through cracks between the curtains, and I get out of bed. I pull the curtains open, and a white light pours into the room and is dazzling me. It has snowed overnight, and as far as I can see, the ground is covered.

I have a strong urge to go outside. It's like someone or something is calling on me in a non-human voice, and, confused with tiredness, I take out an overcoat and a pair of boots. Carefully, so as not to wake Mom and Dad, I unlock and let myself out of the house and start walking over the fields in the ankle-deep snow. The wind is blowing by me in gusts and hitting up under my clothes. It feels as if the cold fingers of a skeleton are grabbing my neck. The snow starts falling again, and the snowflakes that prick my face sting like flying sparks. I'm walking farther and farther out over the fields and near the desolate, snow-covered heath that lies on the other side. Beyond my field of vision I can see formations of small black dots moving over the white area. My feet are changing direction on their own accord.

The air is filling with cries of lamentation and with whimpering as I'm gradually approaching. Two women and a boy are standing, without coats, in the snow. One of the women is tall and slim and wearing a black dress. She is beating on her sunken chest with hands clenched into fists, and the other two are on their knees in front of her.

"We are all condemned to die," screams the woman and beats on her chest.

I'm stopping and watching them, but they don't seem to notice me.

"I killed my husband because I found out he was cheating on me," screams the woman and starts laughing.

"I loved him," says the woman on her knees quietly, "don't punish me. At least, spare your son."

"Go!" screams the woman who's standing and points with her finger out over the heath. "Go and die in the snow."

"You too," she screams and points at the boy who is cowering in a squatting position. "Go and die in the snow."

The woman and the boy are slowly getting up and beginning to walk away in the falling snow, their heads bowed. The woman in the black clothes is staying behind and laughing loudly. She falls down on her knees and lifts her face toward heaven and lets out a drawn-out scream that gives me goosebumps. Then she collapses into a little black bundle that is gradually covered in snow.

I continue across the snow-covered landscape. The cold wind is blowing in on my neck and my face and makes my eyes run with water. The snow crunches under my feet with each step I take because the ground is already solidly frozen. A little farther out on the heath, three small dots are running after a fourth dot, which looks like they're on a chase, without the distance between them decreasing. All four of them are quickly coming closer, and through the blowing snow I can make out a dog that is harnessed to a sled, and three short men who are running after it. The sled is running up next to me and coming to a stop, and the three men surround me. In surprise, I'm looking into three broadly grinning faces. They're round and yellow brown like bronze, their eyes are slanted, and their cheekbones protrude from their sunken cheeks. The men are dressed in clothes of sealskin from head to toe.

"Take me along on the sled," I say.

They quickly look at each other and laugh out loud.

"Where do you want to go?" asks one of them and tries to control his laughter.

"Away from the cold. Out of this snowy desert."

The man bends over with laughter, and the words come out jerkily.

"Haha, then you won't…hehehe…travel with us. Haha haha… well… pooh…all of us together…hahaha…die…aha ah…in the snow."

He tugs at the reins, and the sled starts moving. The men disappear, but their laughter remains hanging in the air. I'm about to turn and walk in the opposite direction, when my gaze falls on the snow, and I feel the hair on my scalp is standing up. There is neither any trace nor footprint of where the men walked.

I'm walking on in the heavy snow, my head pulled in between my shoulders. The cold wind is blowing through my body, and or else it's out of my bones that the cold is growing. When I look up again, I'm halfway inside a circle of people. Some gray-haired old women with wrinkled skin are sitting in front of me. They're wrapped in several layers of dirty and torn rags, but still shiver with cold. My eyes are running with water, when the wind hits my face, and it feels they're freezing into ice.

I take a few steps forward and lean down to the woman sitting in the center of the circle.

"Who are you?"

"We are the last human beings," she says with her toothless mouth, "behind us lies the river of life and death, and behind that, there's nothing."

She falls silent and munches loosely with her pursed mouth. Then she smacks her lips and looks at me with flickering eyes.

"But now it's frozen to…"

Some men who are just as small and wrinkled as the women, and who are also clothed in old rags, come driving a wheelbarrow into the circle. They struggle to push it forward in the deep snow, and several times they stop as if their strength were giving out, but in the end they manage to drive the wheelbarrow in front of the old woman. On the cart lies a man with a gray-yellow face and closed eyes.

"The chief has been killed," says one of the men.

The woman begins to cry quietly while she's rocking back and forth in the snow.

"Who has slain him to death?" I ask.

"The unknown. He almost took the lives of all of us."

"Why don't you try to stop him?"

The old woman gets a hard expression on her mouth and looks at me angrily.

"Who are you who thinks it's possible to stop death?"

There's an ominous silence round me while I'm making my way out of the circle. I'm continuing my walk across the frozen stretch of heath where even the wind has died down. Suddenly, out of the corner of one eye, I see that there is a slight movement going over the landscape. The next moment a black bundle jumps up from the snow, two hands grab my neck, and my larynx is being compressed. Two gray eyes, opened wide and round with insanity, are staring into mine.

I'm getting a grip on the man's wrist and try to force his arms away with what feels like an utmost effort. We're fighting back and forth in the snow while I'm gasping for air. I'm beginning to see black before my eyes when the man's arms are slowly giving way. With my last strength, I'm freeing myself, and the man turns and starts running over the snow at a fast clip. For a moment, I stand and catch my breath before I'm running after him. His dark figure disappears behind a slope, but when I reach the edge, he's nowhere to be seen. In front of me is a wide gray river belt that meanders through the landscape. I climb down the slope and cautiously put one foot on the ice to find out if it holds.

Then I step out on the frozen river and take a few steps toward its middle. Under the transparent ice I can make out the streaming water and a few green water plants that are flowing in the direction of the current. In the middle of the river, the ice has piled up into a gray, grooved edge that I'm straddling with my legs. I'm looking down through the ice, and I see that the water plants on one side of the edge flow in the opposite direction from those on the other side. In a shocking flash that turns everything upside down, I understand that the current in the river is running in two directions. There sounds a slap above me, and then a bang as though the sky is tearing itself loose and crashing down, and I'm being pushed over as the world is coming in through my eyes. A second later all is black around me, and after another second, I see that the universe is lying, like a little shiny pearl, in an indentation of one of my brain lobes. An unimaginably loud bang slams my legs from under me, I feel that I'm sinking, and black water swaps together over my head.

The wetness keeps hitting against my face. I can feel that my cheek is pressing against a cold surface. My whole body is in the grip of cold. With one hand, I'm exploring my surroundings that are smooth and divided into fields. Then I open my eyes and look in on the white tile floor in the bathroom. A rain of water drops is falling down over me, and from up there comes a loud sound of running water. I'm slowly lifting my head, and I'm getting the feeling like I'm moving under the surface of the water as my clammy clothes are sliding over my skin. From a squatting position, I come up and stand upright, supporting myself with one hand on the wall. The cold and hot faucets at the sink are fully turned on, and the plug is in so that the water is running out over the edge. Still supporting myself with my hands, I'm walking over to the sink and turn off the faucets and pull up the plug.

In the stillness that follows, I hear a resonant, metallic sound that makes me think of a soft hum. The sound is gradually growing louder and starts vibrating in my ears. It's a cold and beautiful sound that calls out to me: "Come. Come."

I walk out of the bathroom, through the hallway that's in the dark, and open the door to the lighted kitchen while the sound is growing stronger. I pull open the top drawer in the kitchen table, and simultaneously the song is rising and becomes almost shrill. Without hesitation, I stick my hand down into the drawer, and the vibrations beat against my hand as I close it around a wooden shaft. I pick up the knife and close the drawer and walk back to the bathroom while saliva is pouring out of my mouth, and a sweet, sticky taste of honey is settling on my tongue. I'm standing on the floor and slowly press the knife against my wrist. The sound from the blade is so loud that I distort my face in pain. Then I notice that I stand in water up to my waist, in water that is running in two directions at the same time, in water that's been running in two directions at the same time. The one current is hot, the other current is cold.

* * *

The knife is screaming at my skin while it's cutting into my wrist. A violent strength that's going to split my body apart is pressing from my belly up against a cold spot on top of my head. The strength is running out into my arm and guiding my hand and the knife forward. When the first drops of blood are dripping down into the water, two crossing waves arise in me, and the two currents which are equally strong start pulling in me from each side. The next moment I'm flung out of my body, and, in surprise, I'm looking down from up in the air onto myself. My body is growing smaller and smaller while I'm going up in the air until, down on Earth, I've become a pinheaded dot in size. I'm looking down on myself from God's perspective.

Way out on the horizon, the river is branching out into two rivers that arch away from each other. At first sight, the greatness in that majestic landscape strikes me as overwhelming, next the awareness of my own insignificance takes hold of me. I realize that I'm standing at the outmost boundary. There's only one choice left, all else has disappeared. I can live, or I can die.

Though I didn't let go of it, the knife drops from my hand and hits the floor with a dull thud, and I stare horrified at my hand that is opening and closing convulsively like a claw. The next moment I'm rushing out of the bathroom, jump across the hallway and push open the door to the bedroom. Half stumbling over my own legs, I'm falling in on Dad's bed. He is getting up, confused, and, with a hard grip on his shoulder, I'm screaming to his face:

"You've got to stop me. I've tried to kill myself. You've got to stop me."

He looks at me, puzzled.

"What's that you're saying?"

"I tried to slit my wrist," I scream, "it…it has taken over from me."

I stretch out my arm and show him the small gaping wound.

"You need to calm down now. Have a seat."

He tries to pull me down to the bedside, but I pull myself free and jump up and start walking obsessively back and forth.

"You must call the doctor," says Mom. "I had a premonition something was going to happen."

Dad puts his legs out over the bedside and disappears quickly into the living room while I keep walking back and forth in front of the bed in great turmoil.

Mom lifts her head from the pillow and is slowly sitting up. She puts her hands on the blanket and follows me with her eyes without saying anything.

"The doctor's office will open in half an hour," says Dad and steps in, "and I spoke with a secretary, and we can be the first ones up."

"I'm going immediately," I say and run one hand through my hair in agitation.

I can't wait. I have to do something.

"No, wait, I'll drive you there," says Dad, but I'm running out into the hallway and begin, in great haste, putting on my outerwear.

Dad is coming out to me.

"Wait."

I try to push by him, and he steps back startled.

Out on the street I start walking through the fresh-fallen snow, still agitated. At the end of the street, I'm turning right, continuing down a cross-street. A great tiredness is slowly coming over me, and I'm nearly disappearing into a waking sleep. My body feels soft and heavy, and I have a hard time lifting my legs over the snow. I'm stopping at an intersection and look around me in confusion. What is it that I've done?

It seems like my thoughts have hundreds of years to catch up on, but slowly it dawns on me that I can't remember where the doctor's office is. I'm going from place to place without being able to recognize the streets I've walked almost every day. It feels as if I've been walking for an eternity.

At last, I'm becoming aware of a noise from an engine. At the spot where I'm stopping, a car is pulling up. The door is being opened, and a man who, I gradually grasp, is Dad sticks his head out.

"Sit in here."

I'm sitting down in the front seat, and he's looking at me, questioning.

"I've been at the doctor's, but his secretary said you hadn't arrived yet. I've been driving around, looking for you for a long time. I was afraid something had happened. What are you doing in this part of town?"

"I'm out of it," I say scared. "I couldn't find my way."

"Couldn't find your way," he says and looks at me in dismay.

The doctor is waiting in the front office when we arrive. He is leading us by the secretary, a young, light-haired girl, who makes me feel ashamed because she's looking at me probingly from the counter. The doctor shows us into the examining room and closes the door behind him.

In the examining room, there is a glass cabinet near the window and, along one wall, a black bench with gray paper pulled over it. The doctor is sitting across from me at his desk with a pen in his hand and my chart open before him. He is an older man with gray hair parted on the side, with a regular face and calm eyes. He must have just gotten out of bed because he hasn't managed yet to button his lab coat. Dad has put his hat in his lap and is looking straight ahead. He is sitting behind me, partially concealed, so that I can only see him by turning my head. I'm sitting there with bulging eyes. I'm trying to calm down. Then I begin to sweat with anxiety at the thought that Dad is going to hear everything I'll have to tell the doctor. The word 'crazy' keeps pounding in my head. Crazy. Crazy. The word has come alive. It's like snakes twisting in my hair.

"May I hear what happened?" asks the doctor.

"I can't sleep," I exclaim. "I've tried to commit suicide."

The doctor is waiting for me to keep on talking, and when I don't, he says, "Why did you try to do that?"

I'm embarrassed and so confused that I don't know what to say. It dawns on me seriously for the first time now, face to face with the doctor, what I've tried to do.

"I've become sick from meditation," I say and notice how the words come out of my mouth disjointedly.

"Do you think that's the cause?"

He leans forward and picks up his pen and a form.

"What do you do day to day?"

"Not any…anything," I stammer.

He fills out several fields on the form. Then he looks up.

"Tell me slowly and calmly, from the beginning."

I sit up nervously.

"It…it all started when I saw an ad," I say.

Now I've told the whole story.

The doctor lets go of my arm, and I roll the shirtsleeve down over my wrist.

He's turning toward Dad on his chair.

"We don't know what happened," Dad says, "this morning we were in shock… He… He never tells us anything."

I'm sitting still, listening, while they're talking together in low voices. The only thing I'm picking up are single words and fragments.

"…hysterical…relaxed…fresh air."

I'm in a faraway place. I'm listening to an internal, malicious voice.

"Coward," it says. "Why didn't you do it? That way you'd have been done with it once and for all."

"Hm," says the doctor and turns around and lays his hands on his desk. "I find it hard to imagine that meditation is the cause of your suicide attempt. I practiced it myself for a few years and I can only say it gave me peace of mind."

"What?" I exclaim. "Don't you believe what I'm saying?"

Beside myself, I'm jumping up from my chair. I am looking around the room, lost, and open my mouth to speak. Then I close it again and sit abruptly down on the chair. How will I explain what happened when I don't understand it myself?

He pulls a sheet out of my chart. His gaze glides down over the page, and from there up to me.

"I can see that you were prescribed nerve and sleep medication when you were eleven years old. It looks like you have a predisposition for hysteria."

"No…but…that was something different."

"In what way?"

"It…it has nothing to do with it," I say, "that was something else."

I turn my head and meet Dad's glance. Then I fall silent and look down.

The doctor gets up and walks over to the glass cabinet. He's standing with his back to me and jingling with some instruments. When he turns around, he is holding a syringe in his hand.

"You'll see. I'm giving you an injection so you can get to sleep."

I lower my head and look away, and he rolls up my shirtsleeve and sticks the needle into a skinfold. After a moment, he puts the syringe on a tray and sits down again behind his desk.

"I'm writing a prescription for some nerve medication and for some sleep medication. You'll take two nerve pills three times a day, morning, midday and evening, and two sleeping pills before you go to bed. We're starting with two hundred of each kind. If necessary, you can get the prescription renewed later on."

"For how long will I have to take them?" I ask in a low voice.

"That depends on you," he says.

He looks up and smiles and hands Dad an envelope with the prescription.

"I'm sure that you'll soon be getting better," he says.

Dad picks up his hat and says goodbye. Then he takes me under his arm and leads me by the secretary's counter and out of the clinic.

I have a feeling that the visit went poorly. The doctor must have misunderstood me. He's given me pills but didn't make any attempt at healing me. Perhaps I haven't been good enough at explaining how awful I'm feeling.

But I don't dare to protest. At least he didn't tell me that I had to be admitted to a psychiatric unit.

In the car, we're sitting in silence. A paralyzing drowsiness is gradually taking hold of my body. It's as if I'm bashing my arms and legs under water so as not to go under. The surface of the water is as smooth as sleep.

I'm slowly, step by step, climbing up the stairs, while Dad is putting the car in the garage. Inside the door I stop and sway uneasily. Mom's face appears before me.

"What did the doctor say?"

I'm moving my lips without saying anything. Dad steps up to my side.

"Lie down in your bed," he says.

He lifts me up with difficulty and carries me to my bed. I can sense some fingers that carefully loosen my clothes and pull them off. Then the black water closes over me.

Part 4

In my dream, I was dead. Far away in a room I can hear an incomprehensible voice speaking. Then a door slams, and another one opens. For a while, all is quiet, and there's darkness around me. My eyes are glued together by sleep, and I have trouble opening them. At first, I'm being blinded by the light, then I sit up and run my fingers through my greasy hair. It feels as though my brain has been stuffed by a taxidermist. Why was I dead in the dream? I put the blanket aside and carefully step out onto the floor. I notice that I have a strong urge to pee.

While I'm standing over the commode, I catch sight of the small scab on my wrist, and in a flash, everything is coming back and I'm beginning to shake with anxiety. What is it that I've done? I'm feeling as fragile and transparent as glass. I cautiously push down the handle of the door to the living room, step in and close it carefully behind me. Dad is sitting in a chair by the window. He's watching me without saying anything, his eyebrows raised. I walk in, stiff-legged, and sit down in one of the leather armchairs. The silence is unbearable. "How long have I slept?"

"For more than a day."

I'm embarrassed and feel painfully exposed. What happened is so awful I can't stand thinking about it. Nervously I'm pulling my shirtsleeve down over my wrist. A bit later, the door opens, and Mom comes in and sits down carefully on the edge of the couch. She's rolled up her sleeves and is holding a dish towel in her hand. We are sitting in tense silence without looking at each other. Her face is devoid of expression. Until finally, Dad clears his throat. Mom is looking over at him and says, "You've got to tell us what happened."

"Yes," I say. "It's for your own sake. We have to try and understand." I don't know what to say. Dad may have told her what I said to the doctor. Perhaps she wants me to tell her myself. "I did something stupid," I say. "I...I didn't want to do it."

"You will understand that we are anxious," says Mom. She lifts her head and looks me in the eyes. "How could you do that to us," she asks. "What do you think other people will say?"

I notice that the stuffed-up feeling in my head is going away. "Other people," I say, "is that what you're thinking of?" I stop speaking, and it's quiet. "I've thought about," I say and start shaking with annoyance, "how odd it is that you guys never discovered, while I was a baby, that it was actually a changeling lying in the crib. You could have dealt with me then and there, instead of doing it the slow way."

"What do you mean by that?" asks Mom angrily. I'm bowing my head. "There's something I've never understood," I say. "Why didn't you help me when I couldn't swallow my spit?"

"That's not true," she says, "there was nothing to talk about."

"You must have known that I was being bullied every day. Why didn't you do something? I was only eleven years old."

"Ask your father," says Mom. I turn to face Dad. Neither he nor Mom says anything. "There isn't any answer, is there?" I say. "It's because that's something one mustn't talk about, right. There mustn't be any scandals. So just let me go on."

"You don't understand how worried we were," say Mom and Dad at the same time. We're sitting in silence. The ticking of the clock is in sync with the pulse rate in my ears. I cross my legs nervously.

"There's apparently no limit to what you find yourself having to listen to in your own home," says Mom. She bends over and starts crying so that her body is shaking. "Why does it always have to end up this way?" she asks. She turns her face to Dad. "And you don't say anything, as usual. You can't even put your own son in his place."

Dad is moving uneasily. An expression of pain is passing over his face. "I think more than enough has been said," he says. Mom gets up and is walking out of the living room while she's crying into her handkerchief and angrily talking to herself. She slams the door after herself. Dad and I stay seated and avoid looking at each other. "How are you doing?" he asks.

"I don't know. I thought I'd be doing better after having slept." The strange sensation of levitating, as when one can't breathe, has returned. I'm looking down at my hands that are shaking. "I didn't know that it would go like this," I say. "I didn't do it to punish you."

"I've been at the pharmacy with the prescription," he says, "your pills are sitting out on the kitchen table." I'm sinking. The desire to live, the little reprieve I got from sleeping, is seeping out of me. I wish I was dead. "There's also a letter that's come for you," he says.

"A letter?" I say. "From who?"

"There was no sender written on it," he says.

I'm getting up and walk slowly out to the kitchen where Mom has taken all the China out of the cabinets. She's standing by the sink, and she's not looking up. I pick up one of the two pill bottles that sit on the table and cautiously turn it round and round in my hand. It's the one with nerve pills. I really don't want to take them, but I need them. I take a water glass and I reach over Mom and turn on the faucet. I can tell I'm annoying her. I'm laying the first pill on my tongue and wash it down with water. "What are you doing?" I ask.

"Clearing my head," she says.

Dad comes in with the letter in his hand while I'm swallowing the other pill. "Here it is," he says. It's a light blue envelope. I open it. I have to hold on to the edge of the table to steady myself. "Who is it from?" he asks.

"It's from a woman I don't know," I say and look at the signature. I've never heard her name before. My heart is beating hard. "It's an invitation," I say, "an invitation to take part in a meditation course."

* * *

I'm too nervous to stay in the house, and I take a walk to be alone to think. I'm still upset over the letter. It bothers me that, under different circumstances, I'd surely have been happy to be invited to the course. I wonder whether I'm in the index card collection of Joakim and Louise, and if they've given my address to others. I have a suffocating premonition that I won't be able to break free.

The first pill makes me calm on the surface, but underneath I'm as anxiety ridden as before. The circumstances I see consist of a disturbing amount of meaningful details, but, taken together, it appears that they cancel each other out so that the whole is like an empty, daunting and meaningless form. To go into town is like going into an uncomfortable, cold no-man's land.

Without thinking about it, I've been looking around myself the entire time, looking for something. It gradually occurs to me that I'm looking for those posters with smiling, motherly Indian women or serious, full-bearded Indian men that sometimes hang on house walls. If I see one of those, I'll tear it down. I feel like stopping everyone in the street and warning them.

I still have a hard time grasping what happened, and I find it difficult to recognize myself. It's almost like can't think of it without starting to shake. How could I do that?

While I'm walking, I feel like breaking out into laughter about the most banal things, like that dog that's running, its tail whipping, down the street a bit and stops now and then to sniff a lamppost or the corner of a house. I'm beginning to feel strangely safe as I'm moving, as I'm walking from place to place in the snowed-in streets, until I realize that that is so because it's like a mirror image of how cold and stiff I'm feeling on the inside. One moment it is as if the world will collapse again in through my eyes, and I get so fearful that I have to stand still or sit down on a bench. Then I'm feeling that some uneasy chemical calmness is flowing out into my nerve tracts, and I get up and go on.

My mood is shifting all the time. After I've been anguished, I'm moving into an unusually devilish humor. I can tell that something new and unknown is about to live and take my power away. I hate all people. I'm staring so intensely at a random man in a black coat with a fur collar, bareheaded and with a scarf, who is casually walking in my direction, that he looks up with a surprised expression on his face. As we pass each other, I stick my hands in my pockets and clench them hard into fists in my mittens. I have a crazy desire to hit him in the face with a fist. I want to see his pain, and I want to see the blood as it runs down over his jaw and drips into the snow in a growing circle. I'm going a few more steps, then I can no longer control myself and erupt in loud laughter. I'm the only one to understand that, although everything seems peaceful, an invisible war has broken out among us humans.

My laughter stops, and I'm clenching my fists even harder in my mittens. I can feel that the war is turning in a new direction. It's me, myself, who it's turned against. How has it happened that I've come this far? A sudden sense of shame makes my cheeks burn. I'm feeling possessed, but all the same, what happened is my fault. Why didn't I see through Louise and Joakim a bit sooner? How could I trust them so much? I hate them for not having told me the truth.

I'm getting a devilish desire to go back to the house, lock myself in my room and sink back down into the horrifying subterranean grottoes that are located behind my forehead. I'm regretting that I've taken the pills because they prevent me from experiencing the horror directly. I would like to die. My life is destroyed. I'm frightened of myself, but even though I try, I can't free myself from the thoughts about death.

I turn my collar up and force myself to walk on quickly, my head bent way down on my chest. I have a feeling of being followed and that, any moment, people can start laughing at me and look at me with distorted faces.

Dusk is falling, and it makes me nervous and restless. The light from the shop windows is falling onto the sidewalk, and the streetlights are coming on. I'm getting so terrified that I have trouble breathing at the sight of the receding light, which means that the night and the powers of darkness are approaching. That makes me think of my sleeplessness. It occurs to me that I don't know what will happen tonight. One way or another I must have unconsciously imagined that this nightmare would be over after my suicide attempt and after I've taken the pills. My nervousness is growing. I still don't know if I'll be able to sleep tonight.

When I come back to the house, Dad and Mom are sitting in the kitchen, and both look up but don't say anything. I can sense that they've been talking about me. I go into my room, but I can't stand being by myself, and when I've lain down on my bed, I get up and walk back to the kitchen. I can't concentrate on anything because all my thoughts trigger anguish. As I'm stepping in, Mom and Dad again stop talking. I'm sitting down and have a feeling that I'm ready to talk about whatever, just to break the silence. The words are almost flowing into my mouth.

* * *

"Do you think you'll be able to sleep tonight?" asks Dad.

"I don't know," I say, "I hope so."

I swallow the pills I have in my hand. I'm so nervous that the water is sloshing around in the glass when I lift it to drink. I'm just about to cry with anxiety, and I wonder if it weren't better if I had been admitted.

"I'm so sorry for what I've done," I say.

"You've got to call if you need to," he says.

The night is lying there outside the window, and it looks like dark, streaming water, giving me the feeling that the house is on the edge of the sea. The alarm clock on the table is ticking loudly in the stillness. I'm stopped in front of the bed, silent, full of conflicting emotions, then I crawl in quickly, to get it over with, between the cool cotton sheets and turn off the light. When I close my eyes, visions jump forward on my retina. I open my eyes wide, and I'm lying like that for a long time before I close them again. Although I'm afraid, I do want to sleep, and I let my gaze slide down through the bloody underworld that I've come to know all too well. It appears that the nerve pills I took work in such a way that the anxiety is becoming less present. I have the feeling that I'm at a bit of a distance as I observe the disturbing events.

After a little while, the visions are beginning to press on more, and finally my heart is beating so strongly that I have to sit up.

I switch on the ceiling light, and, when I've lain down again, I pull the lamp over the bed and direct it so that the light shines right into my eyes. At first, I'm lying there staring up into the lightbulb, then I start slipping into seeing the bloody images, and I begin opening and closing my eyes: open, closed, open, closed…I'm lying in the light with blinking eyelids until at long last, in the morning, I manage, with the help of the pills, to fall into a light sleep.

When I wake up, two hours have passed.

I give up and pick up a book, and, while I'm trying to read, I nervously look at the hands on the alarm clock over the back of the book. Then I realize I can't read. The sentences are waving up and down before my eyes, and what I'm reading makes me upset and nervous and gives me a floating sensation as if I were losing consciousness.

I put the book down. Then I pick it up again and try to read one more time. I can't. I who is used to spending most of my time reading: I can't. It is like I misunderstand the author's meaning, or else, he has put a scary and secret meaning in the words. Maybe he meant something totally different from what's on the page. The worst is the word 'crazy'. Even if it's not printed on the page, I'm seeing it behind the other words.

I get up and begin walking around in the dark house. I realize that I must try to acquire new sensory impressions that will divert my thoughts.

* * *

126

The tree stump has a little white skull on the top. Around it are withered, cut branches that stick up out of the snow. Today it's been three days since I attempted to commit suicide, and I haven't done anything but walk. It makes me desperate and fearful that that's the only thing I can do. I'm putting one of my feet on the tree stump and lightly pushing the snow away while I'm looking around. Here it's quite desolate. Through the snow-covered pine trees, I can see a snow-covered meadow in the distance. I'm breathing hard with the effort of walking in the deep snow, and my breath is visible in the air.

In the three days that have passed I have strolled in the dirty snow in town, over the frozen fields and through the snow-covered forests—from one place to the next—randomly, wherever my legs led me. I'm being driven forth by something inexplicable in myself, by a fear of stopping, but regardless of how far I walk, I don't get tired enough to fall asleep in a natural way. Even when I'm in my room, I need to keep walking.

Several times, my body gives in to shaking, or I slide into a floating lightness that makes me think of times when I had the flu as a child and was prostrate in a fever sleep. In the street, I break out in laughter in the face of strangers, and afterwards, when my fit is over, everything inside me shrivels up at the thought that I'm going insane.

I push at the snow on the tree stump and, again, try to understand what has happened. I'm circling around it in my thoughts, and I can hear the echo of conversations I've had with Louise and Joakim. I have a feeling that my life is smashed, trashed into pieces, destroyed.

I put my hand in my pocket and touch the bottle with the nerve pills. I don't dare go anywhere without having them on me. Then I look at my watch. I can't help keeping track of when I have to go to bed. Nine hours to go.

* * *

Judgment Day, Judgment Day, Judgment Day.

I think that that's the word that keeps coming out of Grandma's wrinkled mouth even when it's something else she says.

We're sitting in the warm, dark and overstuffed living room at the coffee table, and I have a sense that I'm gradually dissolving. I can't tolerate being alone at home, and I've tagged along because I didn't know what else to do except to go. I can feel that Mom is observing me, almost keeping a watch, with her gaze, and I'm making an effort to behave normally. I'm convulsively holding on to my cup and cautiously trying the cookies. Before we left, I promised I wouldn't tell Grandma and Grandpa anything. I'm regretting that I didn't take a walk instead. I'm getting ill, hearing Grandma talk.

"…We thought you'd been run over by a car when we couldn't find you," she says. "When we got you down from the attic, you were cold and stiff, and you kept talking about God and skeletons and trolls. Amazing…"

I'm afraid she could start talking about something religious. I don't think that I'd be able to stand that. I'm pushing my chair back and getting up.

"I have to go to the bathroom," I say.

Mom follows me to the door with her eyes.

I have a feeling of having an iron ring around my head and that my brain is pressed together.

When I come out from the toilet, I splash my face with cold water and look at myself in the mirror. There are black edges under my eyes, and they're still bloodshot. It feels as if the iron ring is tightening, and I begin to shake and hold on to the rim of the sink. I try not to take more pills than I'm supposed to. Maybe they're not strong enough? I can tell that the pills make me numb and cause everything to seem irrelevant. Of course, I'm tired from not sleeping, but at the same time I'm manic and hyper. I'm sitting down on the toilet seat, and again I spread water over my face to calm down. Then I walk back to the living room.

I sit down on my chair, and while I'm listening to Grandma and Mom, I try to make a plan how to make time pass. I've walked around so much in the town and the woods that I need to do something else. I wonder if I dare go, on my own, to the nearest city where I've only been a few times. That may distract me and get me to think of something else for a few hours. My thoughts keep causing me anxiety, and I can't concentrate on anything.

"Shouldn't we get going?" I ask uneasily.

"Sure," says Mom and looks at me.

When we have gotten up and are about to say goodbye, Grandma grabs hold of my head with both hands and claps me on my cheeks.

"It's been a long time," she says, "and it's nice that you've come along again. But you look tired. Do you make sure you get enough sleep?"

While she's speaking, I see her mouth moving, and I notice that Mom is watching me. I'm afraid that it will again begin to sound as though there's something else Grandma is talking about.

"Yes," I say.

* * *

As we're getting out of town, it already dawns on me that I shouldn't have boarded the bus. In the waiting room and while I was standing in line to buy the ticket from the driver, I was certain that it was a good idea. The feeling of being shut in makes me uncomfortable, and the monotonous movement from side to side and the noise of the humming engine go directly to my head. I have a feeling of being locked up in a sealed metal box.

The last house in town disappears. I'm moving restlessly in my seat and looking out on snowed-in fields. By mistake, I ended up taking a seat way in the back. It's rocking, and the stuffiness affects me so bad that I'm getting nauseated. I'm looking up through the aisle to the driver and at the few other passengers on board. It's still an hour to go, and I don't know if I can make it. It terrifies me that I can't even take a bus.

I'm sure it would help if I could talk to someone. I could sit and try to talk with one of the passengers. But even if I were getting desperate, I couldn't get myself to do that. Nobody sits and talks to a stranger on a bus. People might get the suspicion that there's something wrong with me. I put my hand in my pocket and touch the pill bottle. I don't want to take another one. I might get dependent on them.

The thoughts are unstoppably sliding by in my head. They circle around death and dissolution. I'm looking out on the fields. Suddenly I can see through the snow and the earth as if the fields are transparent or are being illuminated from below. I can see bones, skeletons and half-decomposed bodies lying in the ground. It's a large cemetery, a large churchyard. I almost don't dare look up because it's like life is like this, filled with cruelty and nothing but death and decay. My mouth is going dry, and I try unsuccessfully to swallow. I have to make time pass, somehow or other, without thinking of death. I start counting distance markers as they pass by, then I look down at my watch and count the seconds. It's still more than an hour to go before we arrive. I'm thinking anxiously about how I'll handle the trip back home.

When we arrive, I get out, relieved, at the first stop. It's the town I have at times thought of escaping to if I had dared. The street I'm standing on is filled with sounds and colors, with people who are moving hectically, and I notice that that distracts me. I hardly know the town, and there is nothing I have to do here, so any street can be as good as any other as long as I can move. I'm walking among the strangers and stop to look at a shop window that's filled with artificial limbs. Then I go left on a cross-street and into a cafeteria in a supermarket where, I recall, I once was with Mom and Dad. I buy a cup of coffee and seat myself at one of the small tables in front of the window. Outside is a pedestrian zone where people are walking back and forth. I'm watching them with a sense of relief at being unknown. The thought that I could meet somebody I know terrifies me. But it's unlikely that anyone would recognize me.

I'm paying close attention to what's going on in the cafeteria, and when I've finished my coffee, I get up quickly so that it doesn't look like I'm hanging out unnaturally long without having anything else to do. I can feel that my face is stiff, and I make an effort to behave like everyone else. Hopefully, it doesn't show.

I'm walking out into the street again, and suddenly, without any particular reason, I'm feeling happier to be alive than I've ever been before. But the feeling scares me too. I don't understand these extreme shifts in my mood.

It occurs to me that I don't know where I am. I went out of the supermarket through a different entrance than the one I'd come in. Opposite the warehouse is a big park. In front of me, and behind the trees in the park, rises a large gray building. There's something threatening about it that catches my attention. I recognize it, like from an unpleasant dream. I start walking over toward the building along a path that runs by a lake in the park. Two older, run-down men with gray skin and beard stubbles are sitting on a bench. They're wearing large coats with holes in them and have a few plastic bags next to them on the bench.

As I'm walking by, one of the men gets up and yells: "Hey, you there! Come on over."

I stiffen and hurry on anxiously. That could be me, sitting on a bench with my life ruined. It must be because I radiate insecurity that they talk to me. If there's an alcoholic, a drug addict, or some other kind of psycho in the vicinity, I know for sure that it's me he picks to direct his insolence at. It must look like I'm an easy victim.

I walk out of the park through a gate at the other end, and I'm standing in front of a large parking lot with the big, threatening, gray building beyond it. I'm taken aback when I discover a sign pointing in the direction of the building, with the words 'Department of Psychiatry' on it. I don't want to go in, but I can't leave well enough alone, and I have a clear premonition that I must head that way. I'm walking in through a swinging door, and find myself standing in a big hall. On the right is a kiosk with newspapers, and along the rear wall there are three telephone booths and two elevators with closed steel doors. In a glass cage, under a sign that says 'Information,' sits a nurse and talks on the intercom. I'm almost certain that the cafeteria is on the left, at the end of the big hall, and when I check it out, I find it, just as I had expected.

It's nearly empty. At a table sits a woman, with her head bowed, and cries. A man is holding her by the hand and stroking her cheek with his other hand. I'm feeling both hyper and sleepy, and I buy a cup of coffee and sit down at one of the tables. I open the sugar and pour it along with cream into the coffee, while I try to imagine what it's like to be hospitalized here. With my inner eye, I can see scary images of crazy people in straitjackets and people with small metal plates on their temples who jump in little jerks like dolls, while they receive electroshocks.

Outside the window taxis drive up all the time to a parking area. Behind the parking lot I can see a high wing of the hospital where there's light in the windows, and all of a sudden, I remember. I don't understand why I haven't thought of it before. It was here that Mom and Dad took me when I didn't want to take the pills.

I can vaguely remember the blinds and the strange pattern of shades that they created on the white wall of the psychologist's office. The psychologist was friendly and accommodating, but I can also recall that I didn't like the questions he asked. He embarrassed me because he kept asking me about Mom and Dad. I didn't know what I was supposed to answer.

I can remember that it was half a year after I'd thrown out the pills. There had not been time to see the psychologist earlier, because there was a waiting list with other sick children who would come before me. However, a miracle had happened which I didn't really dare to trust. I had become normal, not suddenly, but gradually.

I can only remember one visit with the psychologist. Did I go several times? I have a feeling that he wasn't able to help me.

I'm drinking some of my coffee, while I'm speculating if things could have gone differently if I'd been cured that time? Perhaps I wouldn't have been so afraid of coming across as weird? Should I maybe go and see a psychologist now? No. The thought that someone should analyze my psyche makes me terribly uncomfortable. I don't think I'd be able to tolerate it.

I don't understand why it's me, who has always been on my best behavior, who has always been quiet and boring, that fell apart. Am I weaker than other people, or am I insane? I can't see that there are other possibilities.

I'm getting annoyed with myself. I'm sure that it's useless to search back in the past. But I need to try and understand what happened.

The couple at the other table are getting up. The man is supporting the woman who's still crying with a hand before her face. They're walking over to the phone booths to make a call.

I'm getting anxious as I'm thinking how I should handle myself to manage the bus trip back home. I could call Dad and ask him to take me, but I won't do that because I don't want to tell him that I can't manage to ride in a bus.

I get up nervously and go to the bathroom to take two pills. Then, with the artificial carefreeness that the pills give me, I walk back to the bus stop to ride home.

* * *

It's the end of the afternoon, and dusk is falling, when I'm stepping out of the door to the doctor's office. I was at the doctor's to have the prescription for my pills renewed, and while I was sitting with him, I tried hard to maintain a balance between appearing normal and still being sick enough to need the pills. I'm afraid if it's written in my chart that I'm insane, that could hurt me later on. The conversation has depressed me, and I'm exhausted from having to pretend.

The brief interval of time when the light is being replaced by darkness is still a nightmare that repeats itself daily. I have a sensation, like an almost physical presence, that two equally strong forces, pulling in opposite directions, are fighting with each other, until the day surrenders and night takes over, after which, against my will, I'm filling myself with a drunken inhuman longing for my own death. I'm walking with my collar up, my head down.

Suddenly a woman, going in the opposite direction, bumps into me. One of her shoulders rams into my chest, and both of us whirl around in a half circle.

"I'm sorry," she says. She's about to walk on but stops. She looks into my face with knitted eyebrows. "Say…isn't that…" She looks as though she'd met an apparition. "I didn't recognize you at first."

I am looking with wide open eyes into her face but can't recognize her.

"Can't you see who I am? It's me, Susanne. We were in a course together this summer."

A weak, blurry image is emerging in my brain. Then I start laughing shrilly.

Susanne takes hold of my coat sleeve and shakes it.

"Is something wrong?" she asks, scared.

The sight of her strong, slim figure comes crashing down on me. I reach out and grab a hold of her arm. The words burst out of me.

"I'm not doing so well. I can't sleep. Do you remember the woman who had to go home from the course? I'm just like her. I'm afraid I'm going crazy."

"What do you mean? What's happened?"

I regret that I said that. Susanne is looking me up and down, like she's trying to get an overall impression of me. I can feel that I've already said too much.

She says, "Listen, we'll have to talk about this."

She falls silent. Then she says, "Can't you come and visit with me? Do you have my address?"

I shake my head, and she opens her purse and takes out a pen and a piece of paper.

"Here," she says and hands me the note with the address on it.

She looks at her watch.

"Can you come tomorrow at three?"

"Yes."

She takes a step back and again looks at me probingly. Then she steps forward, and I'm involuntarily stiffening as she throws her arms around me.

"Watch out for yourself."

She disappears into the dark street. A bit farther on, she turns halfway and waves, and, in surprise, I wave back.

* * *

The next day, as I'm driving on to the courtyard, Susanne is standing at the foot of the stairs.

The house she lives in is secluded. I drove through a little forest and turned onto a small side street that consisted of two wheel tracks and continued through a gorge with trees on both sides which, after a curve, widened into the open square. The whitewashed house sits in the middle of the square, and it's almost impossible to distinguish it from the surroundings except that the black window frames and the red tile roof stick out.

Susanne steps down from the stairs and throws her arms around me, just like last night, but this time I'm not surprised and don't let it show that I'm not used to being embraced.

I've been relieved to know what I'd use this afternoon for.

"Welcome!" she says.

She leads the way toward the kitchen. One entire side of the house consists of windows, and the walls of the three other sides are painted white. There are only a very few pieces of furniture in the rooms, and our steps cause an echo on the floor. On the walls hang photos and lithographs, and on some of the furniture there are strange objects that look like they were bought in markets in foreign countries. Things are so different that I'm getting a feeling of walking through the nave in a church or through an exhibition at a museum. I'm uneasily looking round for that Indian figure that Louise and Joakim had, but fortunately I can't see it standing anywhere. I've never been in a house that is so alien.

In the kitchen, a kettle is on the stove and sends a jet of steam through the spout. Susanne turns off the gas and takes hold of the handle.

"Ouch, damn it," she exclaims and waves with a finger.

She holds it out for me to see the red burn mark at the tip, and I can't help starting to laugh.

"Are you laughing? Don't you think that it hurts?" she asks.

I'm fighting to get control over my laughter, and her face is turning worried.

"Have a seat over there," she says, pointing at two chairs by the side of a cast-iron oven.

I sit down nervously, and I'm looking at the trees and the snow-covered hills outside the window. It seems as though Susanne is trying to create a comfortable atmosphere. Perhaps that's by design because she has a sense that what I'm going to tell her will be uncomfortable. She's sitting down on the other chair.

I clear my throat self-consciously and reach for the teapot.

"No, let it sit," she says, and I hurriedly pull my hand back.

With a look at my astonished facial expression, she says, "It's not done steeping. Just think how important it is that the small, banal rituals be carried out correctly. We are so busy that we forget to see the big in the small."

She pulls up her legs under herself and wraps her arms around her knees.

"Tell me what happened," she says and looks at me.

My gaze is beginning to flutter, but I force myself to look at her. I can feel the calming effect of the pills. I don't know what she'll think of me once I've told her my story.

"That's hard to understand," says Susanne and settles back. "It seems almost too improbable."

"Well, that's what happened," I say with some discomfort.

She opens a pack of cigarettes and lights one. She takes a deep drag and blows out the smoke.

"Tell me, what have Louise and Joakim done to help you?"

"They gave me those exercises," I say.

"That made it even worse?" she asks. "Didn't they do anything else?"

"I don't know…" I say. "It seems they're so preoccupied with themselves, they don't really understand what happened. Or maybe they don't want to understand. But, of course, you know them as well as I do."

"I stopped after the course. I didn't care for the atmosphere of saviorhood out there."

She falls silent. Then she says, "There's something I don't get. Why didn't you stop when you noticed things went wrong?"

I look down and nervously scratch the back of my hand.

"I was so lonely," I say in a low voice.

"What? Excuse me, I didn't hear what you said," she says and leans forward.

"I was so lonely," I say, speaking louder.

I take a deep breath.

"I didn't realize how liberating it is to be part of a community. I couldn't stand the thought of having to be alone again, and by the time I discovered something was awry, it was too late. I couldn't control it anymore."

I raise my head.

"I should have seen through Louise and Joakim a bit sooner," I say. "I think it's because I ended up in a process that seemed to bite itself in the tail. The more I practiced, the better I felt, and I ended up mistaking that with doing better in general. I couldn't know that I'd go completely overboard."

I stop talking and take a swallow of the tea. I'm feeling awfully uncomfortable talking about this.

"There were a lot of things I didn't understand," I say and set the mug on the floor. "When I spoke to Joakim and Louise about it, they gave me an explanation, most times, that was in tune with what they believe. It's only afterward that it dawned on me that they never told me more than I needed to know. The truth—which would've scared me away—they only told me when it was too late. I've thought that there's maybe a secret behind a guru's power: Seemingly telling everything, but, in truth, keeping more hidden. You grow dependent on that kind of people."

I stop.

"Perhaps, all religion is the art of seduction when it comes down to it."

"What do you mean?" asks Susanne.

"Isn't it, for example, a delusion to believe that a man can die and take our guilt upon himself?" I say. "Maybe it's a way not to have to look reality in the eyes because it's too cruel."

"When it comes to the Indian religions..." I say and clear my throat, "all these phrases that promise inner growth, greater capacity to appreciate life, harmony, happiness, self-realization... I'm sure that all these slogans that we know by heart are false concepts."

"Yeah..." says Susanne.

"When I went out to ask Louise for help, I got the impression in some way that she was envious of me being stuck in that hell. She seemed to imply that I'd been lucky. I found it difficult to understand why we had such different perceptions. If you were asked to explain what self-realization means, how would you do it?"

"Well, it's unfolding all one's abilities in one's personality...like a flower, that opens up," says Susanne and starts laughing as if she wants to put some distance between her words and herself.

"I don't know why there's always this image of a flower that comes up," I say. "But I don't think it has the meaning of something opening up. I think it means that it will wither and die."

Susanne keeps looking at me without saying anything.

"I think it's that unfolding where East and West part ways. In the Western understanding, we conceive of the unfolding of the self through the ego, but in the Eastern understanding, the unfolding of the self occurs through destruction of the ego. It's only through dissolution of his personality that a yogi can achieve a state of pure consciousness, where consciousness is awareness of oneself and nothing else. In the Western understanding, such a man would be declared insane because he is no longer in touch with his surroundings."

"Now it's beginning to be complicated," says Susanne.

"I know it sounds dogmatic," I say, "but it's the only way I can explain it."

It gives me an uncomfortable sensation talking about this. I start laughing shrilly. I have a hard time getting my laughter under control, but when I succeed, I turn to Susanne. "In truth, I believe the misunderstandings run even deeper. But it's best to leave them alone."

"I'm glad I quit in time," says Susanne. "I don't know if the exercises would have had a harmful effect on me."

"Maybe we shouldn't talk about a harmful effect," I say. "In any case, I think it's different for a yogi. For him, this...effect is what he strives for. It's me who protects myself from losing the outer world. What helps to find that, something Louise would undoubtedly describe as fortunate, if it means that you lose your mind and that you become one of the living dead?"

"In any event, something good has come out of your exercises," says Susanne. "You seem changed. I have never seen you so immediately present or heard you talk for so long without a pause. At the course, you always kept to yourself. I didn't know that that was because you were embarrassed."

I grimace.

"I can keep talking and talking and talking," I say. "It must be the effect of the pills. I can fall ill after having someone to talk to."

I'm leaning back and look out into the living room.

"It's strange. Everything seems irrelevant. I have the feeling that I could hang myself, or overdose on pills or take my life some other way, and it wouldn't mean anything. I don't know how to explain it, but it feels like I'm dissolving. It bothers me that I can't sleep, I can't read, I can't behave like I did before."

Susanne begins tapping her fingers on the side of her chair.

"There's something I've been thinking about all this time… If I were you, I'd come off taking those pills. They won't cure you. You only manage to become sedated."

"I don't dare come off them," I say in a low voice. "I can't fall asleep without them. They take away the worst anxiety."

"Could you drink yourself full? It works the same, in a natural way."

"I don't think it would work. Besides I don't want to end up as an alcoholic."

Susanne is getting up.

"Maybe we should stop for today. My husband will come home soon. But I think we should meet again."

I'm getting up. I don't know how to say "thank you" to her for listening to the thoughts I have had while taking my walks.

Just as I get ready to say something, Susanne stops me.

"You shouldn't say 'thank you'. I'm so glad that you've been willing to confide in me with these things. That you've shown me so much trust. Do you have others to talk to?"

"No."

"Then let's meet again, soon."

* * *

Letters have kept coming to me from the whole country, from people I don't know, who invite me to courses on meditation. I can't get used to it, and each letter upsets me und causes me to feel bad, even though I tear them to pieces and throw them away or burn them in an ashtray. It's not just the letters, I don't care either for the thought that I must be listed in the Rolodex card collection of Joakim and Louise. I can't break free until I've cut all connections, and I'm thinking of driving out there again and making them remove my card from their collection. Besides, I have a feeling that I must see them one last time. It bothers me that they may still think that I'll come back.

I'm alone in the living room when the phone rings.

"Good morning," says Louise.

I'm about to hang up; it's only courtesy that keeps me from doing that.

"One moment," I say and go and close the door.

"How are you doing?" she asks when I've picked up the handset again.

"I've tried to commit suicide," I say and clear my throat.

"Oh."

A brief silence follows, then she says, "I'm sorry to hear that. How are you now? Are you doing better?"

"It's pretty much the same as when we talked. The doctor has given me some nerve pills and some sleeping pills. As long as I take them, I manage to get a couple of hours of sleep."

"Then you must be tired."

"No, it's odd. I think I'm getting manic from the pills. But I can't read, and I can't tolerate being alone. I have to keep walking all the time."

"Are you still doing the exercises?"

"No."

"That's still for the best…for a little while," she says.

"I won't go back to doing them again," I say.

There follows a long silence, until Louise clears her throat.

"Now listen. We have a problem. Joakim has taken sick and can't look after the horses. We've had the idea if we can persuade you to do that? It would probably be good for you to perform practical work in touch with the earth."

I start laughing against my will.

"You mean it would be a kind of therapy to look after your horses?"

I'm surprised at the malicious tone in my voice.

"It wasn't meant that way."

She cautiously laughs into the phone.

My first thought is to say no. Then it occurs to me that, if I don't go out there, it means they still have power over me. I have to prove to myself that I can do this. I need to go out to the farm one last time to get closure. And this time it will be the last. Now there shouldn't be, under any circumstances, any risk associated with it. This way I will also be able to talk to Louise about her Rolodex collection and get her to remove the card with my name on it.

Several times I've thought that I'd like to talk with Else. She's the only one I know who may have gone through the same experience as me. When I'm out there, I'll also be able to ask Louise for Else's address.

"Yes," I say. "I have nothing else to do anyway."

"That sounds good. Can you come today already? The horses need new straw bedding."

"Yes."

Mom is sitting on her bed in the bedroom, reading in a magazine.

"May I borrow the car?"

She looks up. "Where do you want to go?"

"I promised Louise to help with taking care of the horses. Joakim is out sick."

"You can't be serious, that you want to go out to those people," she says and closes the magazine.

"Yes, I am."

"You're not allowed."

"I think I have to do that," I say. "I feel that I have to see the place one last time."

"Didn't you hear what I said? Are you completely out of your mind?" she exclaims. "You're not allowed to borrow the car."

I'm walking out with a sense of feeling calm, going back to the living room and open the top drawer in the chest of drawers where I know the spare key is kept. I've picked up the key, when Mom walks into the living room. She's walking quickly across the floor and, before I can react, she has grabbed the key out of my hand. She puts her clenched fist into the pocket of her pants.

"Didn't you hear what I said?" she screams with her face distorted. "Are you completely out of your mind? How can you come up with the idea of seeking out those people?"

I understand her well, but suddenly I can't stand it that she should tell me what to do.

"Damned bitch," I yell, "why do you always have to stand in the way?"

"What did you say? Do you dare repeat that word?"

I take a step forward and raise my hand.

"You're not going to do that," she says in a low, slurred voice, "you're not going to do that."

"No," I say and drop my hand.

I'm running out into the hallway and grab my coat off the hook. It's only when I've come out on the street that I uncertainly look back and see that Mom is on her way down the stairs.

"Come back," she yells in a shrill voice. "You are my child, and you'll still be that even if you run away. Do you hear? I forbid you to take off."

I can feel how I'm blushing, and I'm looking straight ahead to avoid noticing the curious looks from the other people in the street. From a phone booth, I'm calling Louise. I'm about to give up making it out there. I decide to lie because it's too difficult to explain why I can't borrow the car.

"The car wasn't in the garage," I say, "so you'll have to come and get me."

"I'm coming right away."

"You won't pick me up at home. I'll start walking your way."

I'm nervous when, half an hour later, she drives up to my side. I don't know how I'll react when I have to talk with her.

"Your mother called," she says when I'm settled in the front seat.

"She did?"

"Yes. I wouldn't exactly claim that it was a comfortable conversation. She wished I should burn in hell. It's strange. She accused me both of having tried to steal you and of having made you crazy."

I don't know what to say, but I'm surprised. I can't remember that Mom has ever taken my side, and at the same time, I can't avoid feeling embarrassed about what she did.

"There may be nothing to say to that," I say.

Louise turns and looks at me, then she directs her gaze back at the roadway.

"I don't understand why you don't try to act like the adult if your parents can't. Why don't you run away from home?"

"I can't run away, the way I feel."

I fall silent and look out the window.

"It's strange. The worse we get along with each other, the more she fights to hold on to me. Perhaps she's afraid of losing me."

The moment I hear my words, I realize what I've said.

"And I'm telling you, that's going to be the result if you don't decide to tear yourself away."

"Yes," I say, "but unfortunately the situation is such that I can't pull myself together to do what I ought to do. When it comes to things I shouldn't do, it's just the opposite."

Louise turns up in front of the courtyard and parks the car in the snow. I'm wondering if I should talk with her about the Rolodex immediately but decide to wait. We're walking to the outer buildings where the tools are kept, and then she's heading with me to the stable. At the sight of the horses that are standing in their stalls, I stop, scared.

"Are the horses inside? I thought they were out on the grass."

"No, it's too cold. They're only allowed to come out and run down their energy a couple of times a day."

I remain standing, trying to muster my courage. Does Louise expect me to go voluntarily into the stalls to those large, powerful animals?

"Maybe I should leave it at removing the straw in the center aisle," I say, "the horses will become scared and kick if I walk in on them?"

"No, they only become uneasy if they sense that you're afraid of them."

I'm swallowing hard.

"The straw in the aisle isn't so important," she says, "it's rather what's lying in the stalls that needs to be changed."

Louise disappears through the stable door, and I cautiously begin to work. I'm sticking a pitchfork into the stacks of straw while I'm considering how I'll manage to come into the stalls without frightening the horses. Then I start slowly scooping up the straw from the middle aisle and stacking it up tightly on the wheelbarrow, and, when that's full, I drive it out to the meadow behind the stable. Inside the stable, I make sure to keep my distance from the horses.

The work is going more easily after I've warmed up. The sweat is running down my face, and I stop and swipe my arms over it. I'm just about to grab the pitchfork again when there's a crunching sound in the straw. I know, without turning around, that the stallion has shifted position and is standing behind me in his stall. My heart skips a beat, and I'm so scared I can't move. It is as though time had ceased to exist, and I'm only waiting for the horse to kick backward.

The kick is violent and comes from inside myself. Without any reason, my anxiety is over and has turned into courage. I discover that I'm free and can move, and I turn and look at the stallion's behind. At the sight, I start laughing. What is it that I'm afraid of? No physical pain can be worse than what I live through at night when the executioners swing their bloody axes over their victims in my unconscious.

I realize that I—who is afraid of getting dirty—am standing up to my ankles in urine and crap.

A sweetish smell from the damp straw rises and blends with the odor from the horses' leather. The impression of this odor is as though it evokes a memory from the earliest times, a déjà-vu from when I didn't exist yet. I can make out a faint, blurry image, and I remember how the Earth was covered in endless waving grassy plains. A shudder runs over my skin as I'm being taken over by a knowledge that once man and horse were one. That was so according to the myths.

I give the horse a slap on the flank and get it to move over to the opposite side of the stall. It whacks a few times with its tail, turns its head and looks at me with two deep-set eyes that shine in the color of brass in the semidarkness. I'm putting one hand on its damp muzzle and, with the other, stroke down over the white spot on its forehead. Then I take the pitchfork and start clearing the straw out of the stall.

I'm working hard with short, measured movements which slowly give me a new, but also strangely familiar awareness of my body. As I'm standing, leaning over the pitchfork, I notice how my muscles contract and relax, my joints turn easily and frictionless, my bones are flexible and strong. I straighten my back and take a deep, liberated breath. At the sight of the stallion, I laugh so that there's an echo in the stable. There's nothing I have to fear from that one.

In the stall, I stand next to the horse and push it to make room for me to take out the straw. In the last stall, I'm crawling, almost overconfident, in under the belly of the mare to see what she'll do. I'm no longer afraid of anything at all. The mare remains standing calmly. She turns her head in a lazy movement and looks at me curiously with her eyes that shine with a brown glow.

A little later, there's the sound of steps outside the stable, and Louise is walking in.

"Are you finishing up? Don't you think it's getting too dark?"

"Sure," I say.

She casts a look around the stable.

"Come into the kitchen when you're done."

A quarter of an hour later, I put the pitchfork in a corner and walk toward the door opening that shines weakly as a speck of light in the growing darkness. I stop in the doorway and look back at the horses. Then I lower my head and step out into the twilight.

When I've come into the kitchen, I'm sitting down on a chair. I don't know what to say to Louise. I find it difficult to start talking about what I'd like to get to.

"How's Joakim doing?" I ask to say something.

"He's laid up in the bedroom with a fever. Most of the time he's sleeping."

She puts two mugs with hot chocolate on the table, and I grab one with both hands. I'm drinking a bit, and I'm about to swallow it when I pick up its taste on my tongue. It may be my reluctance at being here, and perhaps I wouldn't have let show my reaction to the taste in the past, but in any case, the chocolate is coming out between my tightly closed lips and falling down on the table like a rain of brown dust.

I let on that I'm embarrassed, like I've had a coughing fit, and get up to get a kitchen towel. Louise has stopped drinking and is looking at me in surprise over the rim of her mug.

"Are you getting the flu too maybe?"

"I hope not."

"It does help to drink something hot."

I'm feeling obliged to take another swallow and quickly down the bitter liquid without tasting it.

"What kind of chocolate is this? It tastes different."

"That's because I make it with water and don't add any sugar. It's really not very healthy. But I'd like to give you something hot."

I'm putting the mug back on the table.

"Was it hard cleaning out at the horses?"

"No…well, it was, but I got warm quickly. I don't know why, but I felt in a better mood than I have in a long time…"

I'm amazed that I can sit here and talk so calmly and effortlessly with her.

"There's something incredibly nice about being in the company of horses," she says. "It's not because I ride that much, but I enjoy staying out in the stable with them. At times, I get a feeling of hitting a primordial ground in myself."

"I was feeling like a centaur today," I say and laugh because I can hear how stupid that sounds.

"Horses…" Louise says, thoughtfully, "I heard a story the other day. A man I know through some friends of ours traveled a few months ago to India to visit his guru. The guru is the kind of person who can see straight through people. One day the man wanted to do some mischief to the guru and asked him to let him hear some truth. The guru told him not to let go of the reins… When the man came back to Europe, our friend was out there in the airport to pick him up, and he drove him straight to a mental hospital."

"I don't understand," I say and shift uncomfortably.

While she has been speaking, I've begun breathing more nervously.

"Why did he do that?"

"Don't you get it? The guru could see that the man was going downhill and tried to warn him. But that must have been a truth he was unable to take in. He let the reins slip…"

I start breathing jerkily.

"Do you mean to say a person can go insane from knowing the truth?"

"No, of course not. In this case, it was the guru's clairvoyance that made it possible for him to predict what would happen."

"Well, then I can't see that the guy had any choice."

"He could have stopped letting go of the reins."

"How can you stop that?"

"I really don't know," says Louise and laughs, "I would think that there are thousands of ways which very much depend on the circumstances."

I try not to think about that.

"Have you heard how Else is doing?" I ask.

"No."

"I'd like to have her address," I say.

Louise smiles apologetically.

"Unfortunately, I can't give it to you."

"Why not?"

"We don't pass on the addresses we have."

"I'd like to talk to someone who's gone through the same experience as me."

"I cannot give it to you, unfortunately."

"You guys have given out my address to lots of different people."

"What do you mean?"

"I keep getting letters from people who invite me to courses on meditation. I'd like you to stop that. I'd like you to remove the card with my name from your Rolodex."

Louise looks at me.

"If you think…"

She raises the thermos.

"Would you like another cup of chocolate?"

"No thanks," I say. "I'm not so well. I think I'd like you to drive me home."

"How is it actually going?"

"I don't know."

I lower my head and put my forehead in my hands.

"It feels like I can't breathe."

Louise frowns worriedly.

"I thought that the pills the doctor gave you helped."

"They do," I say, "but I still find it difficult to sleep. Why didn't you guys tell that could happen?"

"Should I call Sten and ask if he can take you into treatment?"

I look up in surprise.

"You'd like to be healthy, right?"

"Sure."

"So, shouldn't I call him? I'm sure he could help you. He's very good."

"I don't know…ok, if it's really going to help."

While Louise is gone, I'm breathing with difficulty. I would so much like to be healthy. The room has begun to sway slightly. Maybe it's the pills that make me sick.

Louise comes back, holding a piece of paper in her hand, "It's so fortunate that Sten has time next week. Here's his address."

I'm pinching my eyes and trying to read the lines that are moving up and down on the paper.

"But he lives several hundred kilometers away."

"Yes, but I think you should go. He's one of the best healers in the country. You really look bad. Shouldn't I drive you home?"

While I'm folding up the piece of paper, there's suddenly a bang and then, a scream. When I look up, Louise is standing at the kitchen table with her hands in front of her mouth to stifle her scream. Her eyes are wide open, in a manner that looks like horror. I look at her in surprise.

"What happened?"

"Call Joakim," she says in a shaky voice.

As I'm getting up, the door opens, and Joakim is limping into the kitchen. He's in his pajamas, and his hair is greasy and messy from lying in bed.

"What happened?"

"Joakim, I dropped a mug. I wanted to pick up the car key and pushed against it," she says in a hurried, nervous voice.

She grabs hold of his arm.

"Joakim, what does that mean? I'm afraid."

He starts running one of his hands down her back to calm her.

"It's not certain that it means anything in particular. You've got to try not to see major disasters in everything that happens. Can you remember what you were thinking about the moment you dropped the mug?"

"No, I got so scared, I forgot…I…I don't know…"

Joakim keeps trying to calm her, and it seems like she's slowly settling down. She walks out to the utility room and returns with a broom to sweep up the shards. I'm getting up nervously and stand by the door.

"I need to lie down," says Louise when she has tossed the shards in the trash can.

She runs a hand over her forehead and leaves.

Joakim remains standing.

"Why did Louise get so frightened?" I ask.

"That was a sign from her unconscious. She must have thought a wrong thought. That's why she dropped the mug."

I shudder spontaneously and lean my head against the doorframe and close my eyes.

"I don't understand," I say, "but I have a feeling that I understand better than I want to."

"The same thing happened when I had my car accident and ended up with part of my thigh amputated," he says. "I was distracted for a moment."

"Does that mean that if you lose something or do something wrong like…like saying the wrong word, it's a sign from the unconscious?"

"Yes, there's noise on the line, so to speak. It shows that there is a rupture in one's psyche."

"Well, I tell you, that's really an impossible situation. Isn't there anything that happens just by chance?"

"Not for the completed human being who is in full harmony with himself. Nothing goes wrong."

My hands start shaking, and I'm breathing in brief puffs.

"But that's outrageous," I say.

"So you think," says Joakim, "because you don't understand. I'll go in and look after Louise," he says.

I'm sitting down. I can't stand being here any longer. I want to go home, but how am I supposed to go about it? It's too far to walk.

I'm not even sure that I got Louise to promise that she'll remove my card from the Rolodex.

To my surprise, Louise comes back a bit later. She's like a changed person and is smiling. It seems as if she's embarrassed and trying to hide what happened.

"Now I'll drive you home," she says and calls out over her shoulder, "Just go to bed. I'll be back soon."

"Here you go," she says and hands me two cards. "Here's your index card, and here's Else's address. You're right. Why shouldn't I give it to you?"

"Thanks," I say in surprise.

On the way back, Louise is talking nonstop as though she has a bad conscience. I'm having a bad time, holding fast to the armrest on the inside of the car door, and answering only in monosyllables. I have a sense that I've seen something revealing.

When we come closer to town, she says, "It's strange. There's a tradition that a disciple finds his guru, but there's also a tradition that a guru finds his disciple. I thought that I'd found you. I thought that you had a great future ahead of you within our world."

"I'm not going back," I say.

"No, I know that," she says.

She is slowing down.

"We've been talking about going to India," she says. "We feel that there's no future for us here."

I feel like a thief when I noiselessly let myself into the house and tiptoe through the hallway to my room so that Mom won't hear me. I'm so nervous that I can't settle down, and I start walking back and forth from wall to wall. The locked room gives me a feeling of being caged inside an imaginary world, and I can barely control my urge to set myself free by banging my clenched fists against the wall, even though I know that it's not the visible wall that's in my way.

It's like I'm seeing cages everywhere. It's as if Joakim and Louise are locked in that cage which is their belief in the completed human being. The thought of it scares me, and it scares me even more to think that I also might have gotten locked in believing in this if I hadn't tried to commit suicide. I'm almost surprised to start feeling sorry for them. It occurs to me that I don't know them at all and don't have a clue as to their background, and it makes me curious to find out what forced them into this inhumane belief. Something must have happened at some point in time that wounded them. I'm sure I'll never see them again except if we accidentally run into each other.

I'm sneaking into the living room to call Else.

It must be her husband who picks up the phone.

"May I speak to Else?" I ask.

There's silence at the other end.

"Who am I talking to?" asks the voice.

I say my name. "I was together with Else in the course last summer."

"I know who you are. Else has talked about you. It was you who helped her when she was in a bad way. I'll be honest with you. She's in the hospital."

"Oh," I say and swallow. "What…what's wrong with her?"

"The doctors think she has schizophrenia. She has delusions."

"I'm so sorry," I say.

The hand that's holding the handset is starting to shake, and I have to steady it with my other hand. "How long has she been hospitalized? Is…is there hope that she'll get well?"

"We don't know."

There's pressure against my forehead and my temples, like my skull is pressing against my brain. After hanging up, I walk back to my room. Schizophrenia. Delusions. Why isn't it me who's going insane? Will I go that way too? Is it only a question of time?

Someone once said that people who are afraid of going insane don't do so. The very moment that thought calms me down, the doubt returns. Is that anything but a nursery tale? Is it anything but a superstition like the one that insanity is caused by masturbation? I stop short and go back to that last word. I've heard or read that a symptom of the insane is that they masturbate all the time. It scares me to discover that I have the urge but can't help it. Maybe it could help me relax and remove the tension in my nerves.

I'm taking a handkerchief out of the drawer, and while I'm walking to my chair, I unzip my pants. I'm sitting down and awkwardly take hold of my penis. As my fingers touch the sensitive skin, a shock runs through my body. It's so sharp that everything hurts for a moment. My penis is slowly filling with blood, and the skin stretches like a smooth casing.

A slight shiver is going through me, and I'm leaning forward in the chair. Then I fall back again and get ready to remove the handkerchief, when I notice

149

that something is wrong. I unfold the handkerchief. It's dry. I've achieved release, but no semen has come.

* * *

"I'm glad that you came along."

I'm driving carefully because the roads are still icy. Low over the horizon sits the winter sun and spreads a jagged circle of powerless rays that are so strong, nevertheless, that I'm blinded, both by the sun itself and its reflection in the snow, and I must slow down even further.

Susanne turns her face and looks at me from the side.

"I'm thinking whether it's not very nice for you to have someone you know come with you?"

"It sure is," I say and quickly glance at her.

"Do you think what I'm doing is right?" I ask.

After the episode out at Joakim and Louise's, I've been in doubt if I should quit. It was first and foremost the thought of Else suffering from schizophrenia, but also Susanne who was telling me that the doctor's pills didn't help, that got me to that point. I'm feeling that I don't have a choice.

"What did your parents say?" she asks.

"Not much," I say.

"What do they think of me going with you?"

"I think they're glad that someone is going with me, and that they don't have to themselves."

"It goes without saying that they don't understand what's happened. I find it difficult myself."

"They sure don't."

"The more I think about it…I could beat Joakim and Louise over the head."

I've told her about the mug Louise dropped and about Joakim's remarks about the completed human being. I've also told her how afraid I'd been of going insane after my phone call to Else.

Half an hour later, we pull up in front of a red brick house that sits in a tree-lined valley. While I'm parking the car, a stocky man with flaming, gray-sprinkled hair that grows around his bald head comes out of the front door.

"I'll be waiting for you out here," says Susanne, fidgeting uneasily. "I think I'd rather not go in with you."

I look at her in surprise. I'd thought she would have wanted to be present in the examination room. I hadn't imagined that she'd be sitting in the car. That disappoints me and makes me nervous. But I don't protest.

I get out of the car shakily and find myself blinded by the light. When my eyes have adjusted to the transition from inside the car, the man on the stairs comes into sight again. He has bushy eyebrows, and a deep blue shade runs round his jaw. I walk up to the foot of the stairs, and he shakes hands.

"Doesn't your mother want to come in with you?" he asks and nods toward the car.

I look at him in surprise and glance back.

"That's not my mother," I say.

Sten leads me through the house and into a room where there are two flimsy chairs and a couch that is upholstered in black imitation leather. I'm sitting down nervously on one of the chairs, and I'm about to begin my report when he raises one of his hands in the air.

"Hold it. I'd like to first spend a few minutes just looking at you."

He's gazing at me for a long time with a dark look with little glimpses of life. I try to avoid looking into his eyes, and I fear the whole time that he'll start talking about my aura or something similar. If he does that, I'm not sure I can handle it. I do wish Susanne was here.

He gets up and begins to flex and stretch my arms and legs. Then he grabs me by my shoulders and bends my upper body back and forth and from side to side. Next, he turns my head in a circle, and after that sits back down on his chair.

"OK, what was it you were saying before?"

I'm telling him what happened, and I'm moving about in my seat with immense discomfort. Sten is sitting calmly and without moving or saying anything and watching me with pinched eyes. He's listening attentively, but it doesn't look as if anything I'm saying makes an impression on him. His calmness makes me so confused that I have to stop several times because I forget what I was going to say.

"I can still only sleep when I take the nerve pills and the sleeping pills," I say and fall silent.

"You'll have to consider that an exercise," he says. "Think of it as something that lies beyond the limits of what we, as human beings, can imagine, but something we can, within those limits, experience."

"Yes," I say after a pause. "That's the kind of thoughts that make me anxious."

"Why are you afraid?"

"Because…" I hesitate, "somehow or other, it's like saying I've been through death. Anyway, that's the feeling I have."

My shoulders start shaking, and the words find their way out of my mouth on their own. "I'm afraid that death may only be delayed," I say. "I have a feeling as if I'm in the process of dissolving."

"You can really get used to thinking along those lines," he says. "Still, you won't find any answer."

"I keep seeing snakes everywhere. That makes me afraid."

"Have you ever really looked at the pharmacy symbol?" he asks. "Why do you think they chose that one? It's a snake that winds itself around a pole. The snake is a symbol of health."

I gasp, and it feels like my pulled-up shoulders are falling in place with a jerk. To my surprise I notice that I'm beginning to relax.

Sten's gaze has not released me. He smiles slightly.

"It's the old story of original sin that you have misunderstood like most other people. According to common understanding, the snake itself is the symbol of evil. But if you read carefully through the creation story, you'll see that that is an interpretation whose only purpose is to obscure the truth. The purpose is to protect the reputation of the being or the power that we call God. In truth, it was exactly the snake that showed the first humans what they needed to do to become godlike. In the meantime, this insight, like all revolutionary wisdom, is so dangerous that the Power, God Himself, had to come down hard on Adam and Eve and drive them into exile as punishment. But the day we humans cast off our bondage and follow the way the snake showed, that day we'll take over Paradise in a coup."

I've leaned forward, looking at Sten in surprise. Either he must be mad, or…it sounds scary and crazy.

"Enough of that," he says and blushes a little in his cheeks, "let's go back to what we talked about before."

He directs his calm, expressionless face toward me.

"What I can see now is that your chakra in your neck—to use that expression for now—has been added a lot of energy. The center is the spot where the word or the narrative is located, and the neck is the body part that connects the head with the body—in a figurative sense, soul with body. There are several nodal points in life where something old must die so that something new can come to life. I think it's that kind of upheaval you've all of a sudden been thrown into. We also call it growing up."

He leans forward and grabs hold of the edge of his chair with both hands.

"Regarding the forces that you find so hard to control…you may as well reconcile yourself to the idea that there's no miracle cure. It's going to take time before you can return to a so-called normal existence. For some of the people who come to me, and some have gone through the same ordeal as you, it has taken between seven and ten years. For some, it never happens."

"Between seven and ten years," I exclaim. "But that's…I'll be thirty years old by then."

I'm so shaken, I don't know what to say.

"Yes," he says, "you'll be functioning normally that way, you're going to be able to read and to be alone, but it's not certain that you'll be able to sleep like before."

"Well, what's wrong with me?"

He waves his hand as if to say, what good is a diagnosis going to be? Then he jumps up.

"Well, that's it," he says, "are you going to pay right away?"

"Yes," I say.

I'm still so upset that I don't react to the brusque manner in which he has wound down our conversation. I had expected that he'd say or do something, but nothing happens. I put my hand in my pocket and pull out my checkbook.

He's following me back through the house and stops, facing me, at the foot of the stairs.

"Come again another time if you need to," he says and shakes hands.

He closes the door, and I turn round to go down to the car.

"It's good you've come back," says Louise as I open the car door. "I was getting afraid I was going to freeze to death if I had to wait much longer. How did it go? What did he say?"

I'm looking at the house through the windshield.

"He was strange," I say. "Nothing really happened. I understand that I'm not the only one. This has happened to other people too. It sounds like he has experience. He said there's no miracle cure. It will take seven to ten years to get well."

I put the key in the ignition.

"I don't understand why these kinds of people always have to talk about a split between soul and body. What do they mean by that?"

"Seven to ten years," says Susanne, "is that the punishment for playing with your psyche."

"Yes," I say.

I'm feeling crushed.

"If it's true."

* * *

It's late that evening. I'm lying in bed, waiting to fall asleep. I told Mom and Dad about the trip, and their reaction was more understanding than I'd expected. I didn't dare to tell them that it might take between seven and ten years before I'm back to normal. My body is strangely, almost unnaturally relaxed, and I'm surprisingly unaffected by the bloody scenes that are gliding by before my eyes. As usual, I took my pills and lay down in my sleep position with the light aimed at my face, and I'm incessantly blinking my eyes so as not to see the visions. I keep thinking about what Sten said, while I'm sliding into a semi-sleep.

A little later the door opens noiselessly, and I'm watching in amazement as a dark figure, in a shadow, steps into the darkest end of the room. I've begun to leave the curtains pulled back because I can't stand the feeling of being shut in, and in the weak light coming in through the window from the night sky outside, the outline of a figure is clearly visible. I'm sure it isn't Mom or Dad. The figure has a flat body, like a piece of cardboard, but its head is spherical. The shadow steps closer, into the light from the lamp, and I can see that it doesn't have a face. I can sense that it exudes a strong radiation of evil. I almost think, no, I'm sure, that it's Satan who's on his way to my bed.

I don't know why I'm not getting afraid. The state I'm in is like a scary dream where you move somnambulistically and unaffectedly through the most awful events. But I can tell it's not a dream. It's something else. I don't know what it is. But I'm awake.

The silhouette stops by my bedside, and I try to raise myself, but discover that I can't move my body. It is as if it is locked. My heart skips a beat but falls back into its normal rhythm when I realize that I'm powerless. The only thing I can do is wait for what the shadow decides to do.

The figure is leaning in over my bed, and suddenly it's sitting on the headboard and pressing its feet against my shoulders. A strong electric shock is running down through my body, and almost simultaneously another current is running up from my lower body. The two opposite currents crash into each other hard. It makes me think of the time when I got a shock, of the sensation of holding on to a live wire unable to let go, until Dad came and cut the electricity. I don't know how long it's even going on when the current from below disappears, and the electric impulses sting as they run out through my legs.

A loud, sharp sound rings out, like from a tight string, and I'm coming to. I'm lying there for a little while, unable to move, then sensation is slowly returning to my body. I'm sitting up. The shadow, as I had expected, is nowhere to be seen. To be certain, I even look under the bed.

My head is buzzing, and I try to clear it. My thoughts are weird and scary as if they don't belong to me. I get up from my bed and start walking around in the dark house. Without a clue why, I'm coming to think about the vision of God the night I tried to commit suicide. In a strange and confusing way, I see the two faces before me, God's and the devil's. It's as though the two faces merge together into one.

All of a sudden, I know who I am. I stop short because the feeling makes me uneasy. I'm no longer the child who's embarrassed and hysterical. I'm no longer the boy who's afraid of being different. I'm nothing. Nobody. In my place, there's a zero.

Part 5

The sound of rain dripping down from the trees has caused me to wake up. A golden light is falling into the room, and I get up from the bed and walk to the window. Outside everything is soaked in water, and small currents of water are running through the snow and collect in large, reflecting puddles, and here and there black, damp dirt sticks out between the shrinking snow drifts. I can feel the warmth from the radiator through my pajamas. It must be the first time this year that the sun is stronger than the frost.

I have a sensation of holding myself in a firm, disciplined grip. In my head, I make plans and create lists for every day to force myself to take on some project even if it feels meaningless.

It still scares me that one moment I'm excessively happy, and the next I mostly feel like dying. If I look back, it seems stupid that I keep clinging to life, and if I look ahead, the horizon appears, no matter which corner of the world I turn to, like a gray, endless desert. I try to avoid looking back or forward, but I'm also afraid of living in the present moment. I have a feeling that I'm outside of time, in a distant, impersonal place from which my own and other people's lives look irrelevant. I can't feel anything, and words like pain, happiness, hatred, love, all the words that are our attempt at expressing feelings, have lost their meaning. I'm living on the most banal of all adages: Time heals all wounds.

When I'm most depressed, I wonder if it's true what Sten said, that it's going to take between seven and ten years or perhaps the rest of my life before I'm well again. I'm getting desperate waiting for something unforeseen or random to happen.

I remain standing by the window, looking out to the sun. Suddenly I catch sight of a figure V, a line of birds flying north. That must be some of the first birds to make the trip this year. I pinch my eyes and look up at that flying letter, and I come to think that those birds are living up to nothing other than the concept 'bird'. They trust in a strong, inexplicable urge inside them, like in a

159

faraway part of the world, that has forced them onto their wings, and they've flown for untold days and nights to get here.

I'm walking away from the window and putting on my clothes while I'm thinking how strange it is that there's that longing that sits behind the birds' chests, that in our system is categorized by the half-derogatory term "instinct." But perhaps man, too, has such a thing as instinct. Perhaps man, too, has this kind of longing to attain his own purpose. Is maybe man's destiny just another word for his instinct?

Maybe it's the weather or it's watching the birds, but with a decisiveness that surprises me, I decide while standing at the toilet that I will no longer make additional attempts at avoiding my fate. For several days now, I've had an almost physical sensation of standing on a height, a wobbly scaffolding, and that I had to crawl back down to earth and start from scratch. If I still have that instinct somewhere back in me, it can lead me to where I can become a human like all others.

The thought animates me and I'm looking at my face in the mirror. I'll try to become the opposite of that completed human being. I'll try to become as primitive as an animal.

After the weird encounter with the devil who came into my room, I've discovered that it is as if my anxiety decreases when I'm looking at myself. I've become two persons, one who observes the anxiety and one who feels it.

I've heard other people talk about having a core, but I don't think any longer that I have one. I think and act and talk, but it feels like I've gone into dissolution, like I'm an accumulation of genes, a collection of cells that could have become whatever. I have a feeling of being liquid as opposed to a feeling of being solid, which prompted me to sign up for Louise's course. But both feeling states are uncontainable because they're unnatural.

During the time I've been taking the pills, my surroundings have come to seem dull and shapeless, and that frightens me because everything is becoming worthless and irrelevant. The thought that I'm wasting my life causes me to feel desperate. I so much want to be well. For that reason, I've started forcing myself to reduce the number of pills. First, I hesitantly discontinued them in the morning when I can best do without them, then I forced myself not to take any until lunchtime, but at night I still can't do without nerve pills and sleeping pills.

While I'm walking out to the kitchen to eat breakfast, I'm thinking that if I could fall asleep just one night without taking medication, I surely could do it again.

* * *

All the snow is gone from the streets except for the embankments that lie over the gutters. From the window of the cafeteria where I'm sitting, I can see the pedestrian zone and people walking by. I've begun to know the town after the visits I've made, and in the cafeteria where I went the first time I came, I'm feeling safe.

Suddenly, while I'm looking out at the passers-by, I'm experiencing an inexplicable happiness that everything around me is real. The feeling is so strong that the hairs on the back of my neck are standing up. It makes me happy that the teaspoon I'm stirring my coffee with is for real, that the cup I'm drinking my coffee from is for real, and that the cafeteria I'm sitting in is for real. All things exist outside myself. They're not something I've made up in my brain. It makes me almost tipsy to be surrounded by physical, concrete reality.

I notice that after I quit taking the pills during the day, I've become clearer in my head. I'm more goal-oriented and ready to act, the feeling of ambivalence is nearly gone. When I leave in the morning, I have put together a plan for how the day should go, but I don't know yet, whether I dare to carry it through.

I keep watching the pedestrian zone, and I have a strange sense that I can see through other people. I think I know their stories. I'm a part of them and, at the same time, I'm separate from them.

It is as though I see things around me in a different way, as if the street is a lit-up stage a projector is aimed at, or as though I'm a child who has only just learned to see. The way other people perceive things is colored by their past history, by their encounters and experiences. Things have a different quality for each person, something is pretty, ugly, or right and wrong. I think that all things have the same properties because the properties they had are attached to who I was before. I'm leaning back and thinking with a shudder of the time my room became misshapen. Of course, I can recall the quality things had, but there's no longer any difference between gold and shit.

It's beginning to dawn on me that I don't believe in anything. I don't believe that the world is layer upon layer of illusions, and I don't believe that any religions, ideologies, or sciences can fundamentally change reality, even if they try.

I've never thought there'd be life after death, but I hope that that's not the case. The thought of paradise scares me, because I've begun to understand that it's an escape from reality. I don't believe that there are several chances, and if there were, I'd feel cheated. The only thing I will do is live. And I've wasted enough time.

After having been close to death, I have begun to understand that it's nothing to be afraid of. Rather it's a kind of certainty, an assurance that my life will not go on in all eternity. Maybe it's for this reason that I'm no longer afraid of darkness either. Darkness is no more than dark, and what exists in the darkness are my own imaginations, my own anxiety.

I have a sense that life is meaningless and unfair, and that my actions take place detached and independent of each other. I can see neither a pattern nor a unifying principle for the life that I've lived, and I still don't understand why I haven't gone insane like Else. Life appears like something impersonal that can be both good and beautiful and ugly and wrong depending on my abilities and attitudes. I'm overwhelmed by a feeling that life will always be bigger than me.

A bit later, I'm interrupted in my thoughts as a cold draft hits me when the door opens. I'm looking in the direction of the entrance to the cafeteria, and I see that two girls are on their way in. The one girl is average, but there's something about the other that I can't pull my eyes off her. I think I've seen her before, but that can't be true. There's something lively and free, but also lonesome and desperate about her that I can't explain. Perhaps it's the way she moves. She has a suitcase in each hand.

I'm watching them curiously for a while, then I get up and get a paper from the rack that hangs on the wall. On the days I'm doing best, I've begun to be able to read again, but I still can't tolerate being alone or sitting still without losing it. I open the paper, and I'm pleased to see nothing but what's written there.

While I'm reading, I'm thinking, at the same time, of my plan. I have a feeling that I need to do something of the kind I haven't done before, because it had been forbidden. The only thing I have to do is catch the bus home by twelve o'clock.

I let my gaze glide over the pages in the paper. That way my eye catches an ad that's on one of the last pages. I'm reading it once and notice that it excites me. Although I know that it's not the right thing to do, it feels like it's the answer to some thoughts that have for a long time been piling up in my head, but which I've only been half-aware of. I'm checking what's on the backside. It's nothing important. Then I look around in the cafeteria. There's nobody who pays me any attention. I carefully tear the ad out and put it in my pocket.

When I look up, I suddenly get the sense that the girl has seen what I did. She and the other girl have gotten up, and for a moment I think that her gaze is resting on me before she looks away. I'm blushing slightly.

It starts getting dark. I'm putting the paper back in its holder, and I walk out into the street to continue with my plan. A little way off I catch sight of the girl who's carrying the suitcases.

All of a sudden, I get an impulse to walk over and speak to her, even though, in reality, I can't get myself to do that, and I'm thinking that I'd never have done something like this before. She has shoulder-length brown hair and is wearing an old leather coat that is a little too short, and washed-out jeans and flat-soled boots. She walks a little bent over as if to hide the fact that she is very tall. I'm walking behind her, arguing with myself. If I'm in the process of changing myself, as I insist on doing, I must dare to follow my impulses. I'm trying to convince myself that the worst that can happen is that she rejects me, but nonetheless I'm scared. I'm sure that for other people it would be easy to do.

I'm forcing myself to walk up next to her.

"Excuse me," I say and hear that my voice is trembling, "I was sitting near you and the other girl in the cafeteria. May…may I help you?"

She turns her head and looks at me in surprise. She looks different, more formidable than I thought in the cafeteria, and I'm regretting that I spoke to her. I'm sure she'll say no.

"Yes, thank you. Really?" she asks and smiles.

"Yes," I say and smile back, surprised and tentative.

She hands me one of the two suitcases.

"It's not much farther."

We're going down the street. I, the awkward boy, am going down the street with a girl. I can't think of anything to say. She's looking at me, searchingly, from the side.

"Do you live here in town? I think I've seen you before."

"No."

I'm looking at her, hesitantly.

"But I've been here a few times. I live in a village not far from here."

We're turning into a side street, and she stops in front of a large, older, dilapidated house.

"This is where I live."

I'm both relieved and disappointed.

We climb up three floors and stand at the end of a long, narrow hallway with a row of identical doors.

She unlocks a door in the middle of the hallway. Embarrassed, I'm following her into the room that must be semi-dark even in the middle of the day, because there's a house in back that blocks the light. Few pieces of furniture are standing about on the floor.

"Thanks for your help," she says and turns on the light. "Just put the suitcase there." She hesitates. "I'm just coming back from a trip, so I don't have anything I can offer you. Do you feel like tea or coffee? That's pretty much all I have."

I feel like saying yes, but I notice that I wouldn't dare to get involved in a conversation, because I wouldn't know what to talk to her about.

"I'll have to go."

"Well, ok. Thank you for the help!" She smiles and seems confused. It appears that she's about to start laughing at me.

I rush out the door so fast that I'm stumbling over my own legs. Her nameplate hangs on the door, and I manage to see that her name is Helene. At the bottom of the stairs, I stop. My heart is pounding hard. I'm feeling relieved that I've broken my isolation, but like an idiot for not having had the courage to stay. For a moment, I think that I could visit her again. Then I open the front door and step out onto the sidewalk.

I wish that Susanne was here, or someone else I could talk to. I've never been in a restaurant before because Dad thinks it's too expensive and the food too poor compared to what we get at home, and I have an almost sinful feeling about having gone into the restaurant and that I'm going to have to spend so much money on food. I remain standing inside the door until a waiter comes and seats me at a table. I sit down and look at him uncertainly, because I've heard other people talk about impudent waiters, and how one is dependent on their whims. It's Susanne who had me go into the restaurant. She says that I must keep in mind that the waiters work on our behalf, and that I should simply behave normally and be myself.

I'm contemplating how one is oneself, while the waiter is handing me a menu. It makes me nervous that he's standing there, waiting. I let my eyes run down over the pages and find the cheapest beef dish. We usually don't eat that kind of meat because Dad can't chew it with his teeth missing. I place my order and hand the menu to the waiter. When he has jotted down my order, he hands the menu back to me. I look up at him in confusion. It was going so well. Is he making fun of me?

"The wine list, Sir," he says.

"Oh, it's the wine list."

I didn't know there was such a thing. It must have escaped me that he switched the menus. I order the cheapest house wine.

"A half-bottle?"

"A whole one," I say.

I'm still not sure whether I'll be able to accomplish what I've planned unless I've had something to drink first. But I'm feeling surprisingly clearheaded in contrast to the stuffy feeling that I used to get from the pills.

The waiter leaves, and I look around the place. There aren't a whole lot of people. Most are busy talking with each other. I pick up the ad and read it slowly. Even if I'm not well and can't sleep without taking pills, I think it sounds like a good idea. I decide I'll ask Susanne what she thinks.

The waiter comes with the food, and when I've put the ad back in my pocket, I'm eating and drinking thankfully, while I'm going over my plan for the evening.

I've begun to realize that I can no longer live by Mom's and Dad's rules. The only thing I wish for is to be free of their values and opinions and to find my own. It has also begun to occur to me that they'll always be right, no matter what I say or do. If you close your eyes and keep the world around you out, then there exists nothing else but what reinforces itself, and I can't pretend any longer that the world around me doesn't exist.

Mom and Dad have firm rules for everything which can be arranged accordingly, and, if something sticks out, it will be brutally cut off or condemned. If I want to come out of this ahead, I must find my own rules and live by them. It's them who are afraid of their surroundings, of anything that's different, and I'm certain that they've transmitted their fear onto me. I want to get dirty and come down to where life is primitive and imperfect. I've been tidy and clean for far too long. I will have to hurry if I'm to catch up with what other young people my age have experienced.

I can remember that Mom used to calm me down on the kitchen table when she had washed me. Then she got me to sing—always the same song with a refrain I didn't understand.

Be-Bop-a-Lula she's my baby,
Be-Bop-a-Lula she's my baby[2]

I sang time and again while pulling down, in embarrassment, the woolen undershirt I was wearing. When I was done singing, Mom would clap her hands. She'd blush in her cheeks and start laughing in a strange and loud manner. "Look at his little thing," she'd say and slap her hands over her face.

I'm convinced that, if I want to get well, I'll have to overcome my feeling of guilt.

I've enjoyed my meal, and I made it last an hour, and I pay without problems though at first, I had trouble catching the waiter's attention. I'm a little tipsy and go out into the street again. It's grown dark, and the streetlights and the neon light on the storefronts have come on. I keep going down the street, and as I'm passing a bar, I decide to go in. It's full of people who are talking loudly with each other, and the music is noisy. Uncertainly, I order a beer. Next to me are a young man in a leather jacket and a girl with short hair.

"It's damned hard to live," she says.

"Yes, by God, it's hard," he says.

She shakes her head and clicks her tongue.

I'm thinking carefully while I'm taking money out of my wallet and putting it in my pocket so that it's easier to get at. Then I drink yet another beer to gather courage before leaving the bar. I'm continuing on down the street

---

[2] English in the original.

where, from a distance, I saw some neon lights and signs during one of my previous visits. In embarrassment, I'm looking at the windows out of the corner of my eye, and I'm afraid to stop. There are mostly men in the street who are walking with their heads held low or who are staring stiffly straight ahead. Every time I pass one of them, I look down. I'm surrounded by what Mom and Dad have warned me against, the sin, the filth, and the guilt behind it, and I'm tingling on the inside with anxiety and tension.

As I'm walking by a tavern, two men are falling out of the door. They start to fight on the sidewalk, and more men are coming out. Normally I'd have hurried away, but I stop and watch. I can feel that the violence excites me and helps me feel close to life and reality, and there's a tingling of tension in my scalp. I'm not feeling afraid, and I no longer fear the pain if they were to beat me up. It's not the physical pain that hurts. They can't do anything to me because I'm in a safe place overall.

At the same time, I'm shocked at myself. I sense that I ought to keep away from violence, but I can no longer see what's right and wrong.

Soon after, the fight peters out without any of the men having come to harm, and I'm walking on.

A bit in front of me, a light-haired girl in a short fur coat steps out under the streetlight. She's heavily made-up, with red lips and blue eyelids, and wearing tight pants and high-heeled shoes. I'm suddenly afraid. I'm trying to pass her, but she doesn't move, and I stop.

"Are you coming up?" she asks and gestures with her head.

I'm trying to overcome myself and my feeling of anxiety. Somewhere back under the exaggerated make-up, I think that she looks young and vulnerable, and I nod. We start walking down the street in silence, and she stops in front of the door to a dirty, gray building where the paint is peeling off the façade. I keep telling myself that I mustn't be afraid.

She walks in through the portal, and I manage to cast a surreptitious glance up and down the street before I nervously follow her. Our steps echo in the hallway where the walls are covered in layers of dirt. A young guy in hole-covered jeans and a leather jacket is sitting on a ledge and sleeping with his head resting on his arms. On the next floor, there are two heavily made-up women, one of whom only wears panties and a bra. They're so busy arguing that they don't look up as we're walking by, or maybe they're so used to men going up and down the stairs that they've stopped taking note.

On the third floor. I uncertainly step after the girl into a room that's lit by a naked lightbulb. The room is empty except for a sink and a mattress on the floor in one corner, covered with a yellow terrycloth blanket. The girl is beginning to take off her clothes with what look to my eyes like well-practiced movements, while I'm nervously looking on, not knowing what to do.

"Don't you want to get out of your clothes?"

I'm fumbling with my belt buckle. The pants fall down around my ankles while I'm taking off my jacket. I'm self-consciously aware that in my confusion I'm taking off my clothes in reverse order. I'm stepping out of my underwear and turn to the girl. She's keeping her t-shirt on, and I decide to do so too. She pushes me to the side with her hand on my shoulder and straddles the sink.

"I'll just have to wash myself."

While I'm waiting, my heart is beating hard inside my shirt. A stream of white foam is running down into the sink, and I can't help thinking how much semen must have run out of her belly. If I feel sorry for her, I'm not sure that I'll be able to perform. Hopefully I can get an ejaculation. I'm nervously thinking what Mom and Dad would say if they saw me here. I can feel that my abdomen is contracting.

"Now it's your turn," she says and steps away from the sink.

I'm drying myself with the wet, used towel and she has me lie down on the mattress which feels clammy against my skin. She's kneeling down next to me and is slowly lowering her head over my lower body. I lift my head and see that she's closing her lips around my penis, which, to my relief, is filling with blood. A condom that she'd kept hidden becomes visible between her fingers. She puts the plastic skin in place and wets it with spit.

The girl lies down underneath me on the damp mattress. The smooth, cool fabric of her shirt is rubbing against my skin as I'm slowly sinking down on her. She takes hold of my penis, and I notice to my surprise that she twists it like it was a handle. I'm gliding in the last bit, and, for the first time I can feel how that soft, folded flesh is giving way, as I'm gradually moving into her. Then I cautiously start moving while her vagina widens until it encloses my penis.

I am disappearing in an unknown and powerful state of excitement that causes tiny sensations to run up and down my spine when it feels like her mucous membranes are retracting. I'm trying to push hard into her vulva and get a strong sensation that I could just as well be screwing a hole in the ground. A dangerous burst of laughter is pushing its way through my neck, but just as I'm about to laugh, she begins with a sudden force pushing her abdomen up and down. I'm so amazed that I can't move, and I leave my hand on the crackling fabric that covers her breasts. If I weren't lying here, in the center of the action so to speak, I'd think the movements she makes are impossible. It seems as though she is equipped with some extra muscles in her back that make it possible for her to heave her abdomen up from the mattress and chop it out of the air even though I'm lying on top. The only thing I can do is push again hard with my hips.

A little later, I get the idea that it's not muscle contractions but a kind of wings that give her this bodily agility.

The thought hits me almost in step with my ejaculation.

"My God," I groan internally, "that's a fallen angel I'm screwing."

The girl pulls herself out from under me, and I'm raising myself halfway on my elbows while I'm looking at her face. She nods in the direction of the sink.

"You can wash up if you like."

I don't know if I should feel relief that it went so painlessly or disappointment that I didn't feel more.

As I'm standing at the sink, I pull the glistening condom off and hold my penis under the running water as I see, to my relief, that small strands of semen hang from it. I also was able to feel that I came. I bend over and wash myself with soap. I have the feeling of being in a movie, and I turn to the girl who's putting on her clothes.

"Now all that's missing is that I collect my money," she says and sticks out her hand.

* * *

The sun is shining in through the window, and Susanne is sitting with half her face in the shade. Her husband whom I still have just barely said hello to because he's almost never home when I visit, is sitting in the living room and watching TV. I can't find out whether he leaves us alone because Susanne has asked him to.

"What's new?" asks Susanne.

"Nothing has happened," I say, "but I've thought I'll try and stop taking the pills. I've decided I'll do that tonight."

Susanne is smiling.

"That sounds really good," she says, "but I didn't think you could do without them. I…I just don't know what to say."

"I need to move on," I say. "I've thought so much about what happened. It leads nowhere."

She's taking a pack of cigarettes that's on the table and tears the tin foil up. I'm looking at her until she's managed to light a cigarette. In the time I've been here, she's been surprisingly quiet, and she's smoking more as if she's nervous.

"I could just as well not exist," I say, "it's like I'm invisible."

Then I fall silent because that is difficult to explain. It can easily sound as though I'm taking myself overly seriously.

Susanne is slowly blowing the smoke out through her nose. It's waving up into her face, and she's pinching her eyes shut.

"I hadn't dared to say so before," she says, "but I'm not sure that I could have handled that without going insane. I think you'll be learning to live in the real world."

"Yes," I say. "Even though I'm still not well, I'm tired of waiting for something to happen. It's up to me myself to get things to happen."

I stop.

"You know who you are, and most other people also know who they are. But who am I? Nobody. I think I'm ready to do almost anything to become someone. If I could become a different person, I'd do anything to do so. But I've discovered that I can't. I must accept myself, even though it's hard."

Susanne blows out a cloud of smoke.

"What are you trying to say?"

"I don't know," I say and run a hand through my hair. "That there's too much pain involved in being a human, but that I have to live with that pain."

Susanne takes another drag at her cigarette.

"I can remember," I say, "that in one of the books I once read there was a description of a breed of goats…"

"A breed of goats," she says and smiles.

"Yes," I say. "In that breed, the bucks have large, curved horns that can get worn down when they fight with each other. But if a buck doesn't make it into fighting, the horns start growing, and since they're curved, they curve into the forehead and bore through the skull and kill the buck. He has to fight so as not to slay himself. I thought that something similar can apply to a human being, but maybe the difference is that we are not determined in the same way by nature. We can decide for ourselves how we want to use our powers."

I'm looking at her.

"I could perhaps understand why I got sick if I'd taken LSD. But I didn't take any drug. It's as if the poison comes from inside my own body."

"What about Joakim and Louise?" says Susanne. "And what about your parents? Don't they have some responsibility?"

"Yes," I say, "but I can't keep piling guilt on them. I've thought that if I take responsibility myself, I may be able to transform the poison into a kind of medicine. It may be a question of the right attitude. I think it's up to me to get well. I don't know how to explain it, but it's like having received a dangerous gift. I have to turn things upside down. I must force the devil to be God."

I put my hand in my pocket and take out the ad and push it over to Susanne.

"What's that?"

"An ad I tore out of a paper."

Susanne puts on her glasses and reads it.

"I've been thinking about that," I say. "But I don't know if it's a good idea."

"It sounds like a good idea," she says. "But have you shown this to your parents?"

"If I want to go through with it, it will be necessary to do it without telling them," I say. "Otherwise, I'm not sure I'll be strong enough. I think they'll try to prevent me from doing it."

She takes off her glasses and pushes the ad back to me.

"I'd like to support you," she says.

"I know well that I'm not healthy," I say, "but I have a feeling that I have to do it."

Susanne hesitates. "It may be very good that it's happening."

"What do you mean?"

"The whole winter, we've seen a lot of each other. My husband has begun to complain that I see you too often."

"What!" I exclaim.

"I think he may be right."

I'm grabbing on to the edge of the table with both hands.

"Are you letting me down?" I cry out and notice that my heart is beginning to beat hard with anxiety.

I don't understand.

"I don't know any longer how our relationship will end," she says. "Or, rather, I'm afraid I only know only too well how it will end."

"I know that I'm much younger than you," I say, "but I didn't think that you found it hard to overcome conventional norms."

"Well, it's not that. Can't you understand that, if it ever went as far as I'm afraid it might, I'd feel like I'm going to bed with my own son? You must understand that you're not as repulsive as you think yourself."

I'm about to say something but stiffen. At the sight of the ominous expression on Susanne's face, I'm scared and lower my head.

"You mustn't take it that way," she says. "Look at me."

I lift my head with an effort.

"Don't you understand," says Susanne in a calm voice, "that I'm afraid that you'll become dependent on me? You're going to have to set yourself free. You mustn't start relying on me."

For a moment, I have a feeling like I hate her, but even though the thought is nearly impossible to bear, I'm simultaneously impressed that she is trying to push me from her. Somehow or other, she strikes me as mature and very responsible.

A little later I'm getting up and put the chair under the table. When I'm about to open the door, Susanne steps up to my side. We uncertainly embrace each other.

"I know that you should try to fall in love," she says. "That's what you need. It will give you something else to think about."

"And how should that happen?" I ask and laugh out loud.

"It will work," she smiles, "when it's me who's sent you away."

"We won't stop seeing each other," she says, "I just think we'll do so a little less often. That will certainly reassure my husband."

I open the door.

"Will you try to do it tonight?" she asks.

"Yes," I say hesitantly.

While I'm walking to the car across the open square, I look back. Susanne is raising one of her hands in the air, then drops it slowly. I force myself to lift my hand and wave back.

I'm still upset over the farewell with Susanne.

It's late in the evening, and I've talked Dad into playing cards. We've been sitting at the table for several hours while Mom has been sitting under the lamp, sewing a pillow for the couch.

I keep thinking about what Susanne has said, and even though I'm nervous and afraid not to see her as much as before, I'm sure she's right. I must not come to depend on her.

It's past midnight, and Mom has gone to bed long ago, when Dad is getting up. He stops at the door and turns. "Is something wrong? You seem nervous tonight."

I'm looking up at him. "I've decided not to take any more pills."

"Do think that's smart?"

"I don't think I can get well if I keep taking them."

"Fine. But you know you can always call if you think you need them."

I'm nodding anxiously.

I look at him as he's standing in the doorway. It occurs to me that he looks old and that he could die.

I'm going to my room. I notice that the courage I've been trying to muster is just about to evaporate. I wonder if I should wait for another evening when I'm less riled up. But I've made my decision. I have to do it, otherwise, I may not dare to do it some other night either.

For a while, I'm circling nervously on the floor. I'm afraid of lying down to sleep, and I have to will myself to take off my clothes. I'm trying to kid myself into pretending it's just a regular evening when I've taken my pills, and I set the alarm as I used to. Then I go to bed. As soon as I've laid my head on the pillow and closed my eyes, the first visions come into view, with a power they haven't had since the night I tried to commit suicide. I've become so used to the sedating effect of the pills that I didn't expect the visions to be so powerful and fear-inducing.

I can see a green, scaly, phosphorescent snake as it is slithering through the empty eye-sockets of a skull while it's playing with its tongue on the scalp. Then it glides down into a grotto where several barbaric-looking men are thrusting bloody swords through the bodies of unsuspecting women. I'm lying motionless and reviewing anxiously what I've learned. I don't understand why it's always this kind of bloody violence I have to watch.

I can't fall asleep. It feels as if I'm being sucked down, and I'm sitting up fearfully.

When my breathing has become calmer, I lie down again and pull up my legs against my chest. My eyes are staring at the bulb in the bedside lamp, and I'm blinking with my eyes, while I'm forcing myself to look down at the horrifying activity in the grotto and the adjacent passages.

"I don't want to take the pills. I don't want to take the pills," I'm repeating to myself.

But I can't fall asleep.

The shrill sound of the alarm clock makes me open my eyes.

Half-asleep, I'm reaching out my hand and am about to pull the pillow over my head, but I'm awake. The alarm clock shows it's seven o'clock, and I realize that I must have slept a few hours without the effect of the pills, but I have no memory of having fallen asleep. Then I swing my legs out over the bed and sit on the edge with a feeling of happiness. I'm feeling light and clear in my head. At that moment, as I put my feet on the ground, I know that a day must come when I can handle no matter what. I'm putting on my clothes and take the ad out of my pocket. Today, I think I'll be strong enough to do it. Then I open the door and walk out to the kitchen.

"I did it," I say to Mom. "I've slept the whole night without taking pills."

* * *

Instead of looking up the address in the ad, as I'd planned, I'm standing in front of the door to Helene's room. I have plenty of time and, as I'm in town anyway, I may as well first visit her if she's home. It's an impulse the relief over having slept a whole night without pills has given me. Ever since that first evening I have thought of visiting her, but until today, I didn't dare.

Uncertainly, I take a deep breath and knock on the door. A chair rattles inside, and the door opens, and a young guy looks out. Surprised and disappointed, I take a step back.

"Yes?" he says.

I hesitate because I don't know what to do. Then I say, "How come I don't see Helene?"

"Helene? She lives next door."

He points at the little nameplate that hangs on the hook on the door.

"My name's written right here."

He closes the door. I can't make up my mind if I should take off or knock on the next door. The easiest would be to retreat. I slowly turn and walk toward the staircase. At the top of the stairs, I stop. Then I'm walking hesitantly back through the hallway. I'm making sure it's Helene's door I stand before, and I raise my hand. I'm about to strike my wrist against the doorframe when I stop again. My arm drops. Then farther down the hallway, a door opens, and it's like a circuit blows in my head, and without me consciously moving it, my hand shoots forward, and I knock on the door twice.

"Come in," says a voice.

I cautiously stick my head into the room. From the opposite end, Helene looks up in surprise. I hope she can recognize me.

"Is that you?" she asks. "Come right in."

I take a step into the room and stop. "I'm not bothering you?"

"No," she says.

But I can tell she's still surprised.

* * *

I'm sitting on Helene's couch, looking through a magazine while I'm waiting for her to finish taking a bath. I'm still astounded that that I've gotten the better of myself and come to visit her. I ought to get moving on the business with the ad, but though it's late afternoon, there's enough time, and I can do it later.

Helene has been talking nearly nonstop while I've been here, only interrupted by some sudden outbursts of laughter, and I didn't have to say much at all. At one point, she asked me what I'm doing, and after some hesitation I told her I was thinking of studying Danish, I can't imagine what I'd be doing otherwise. Studying is the only thing I know how to do. I turn a page in the magazine and think about how my emergency lie could turn into a truth if I decided to sign up at the university. I don't know yet if I could manage to study that much, but it would be a way of returning to a normal existence.

Helene is smiling as she comes into the room. She's wearing a white bathrobe and has a towel wrapped as a turban around her hair. She lets the bathrobe slide down from her shoulders, and it falls on the floor. I nervously pretend that I'm reading while I can see, over the edge of the magazine, that her body is slim and still a little tanned from last summer. She's leaning forward and drying her hair with her head down, and then she's putting on her clothes with her back to me.

"Don't you feel like staying for dinner?" she asks while she's stretching her back. "I have a bottle of wine."

I look at her in surprise.

"Yes," I say and clear my throat, "I'd love to. But then I have to call home first."

"There's a phone booth down at the corner."

When I come back after my phone call, Helene has set the table and is sitting on a chair, her legs crossed, smoking a cigarette.

"Is it ok?" she asks and shakes off some ashes.

"Yes," I say and sit down across from her.

I'm not telling her about Dad's reaction and his question about what I'm doing.

"I don't know why," she says, "but I have a feeling like we're both on the run."

"No," I say and hesitate, "I'm not on the run."

She's taking a piece of bread over to her plate.

"So, I've just got to speak for myself then," she says. "I took off when it became too much."

"To here?" I ask.

"No, abroad."

She picks up two glasses and blows the dust off them and holds up the wine.

"I responded to an ad that had been placed in a paper by a hotel owner who was looking for young girls. I thought that I'd be working as a waitress in a restaurant, but I found out that I'd been a little too naive. I was being employed to be a barmaid at a nightclub for businessmen. The place was called 'Club Artemis'."

She shudders.

"We had to walk around in short skirts while serving, and there were mirrors on the floor so the men could see up under the skirts. I don't know how many times I had to slap a guy because he would come on to me."

I can sense that a distance is coming between us. I can feel my lack of experience, and that causes me to look at her vaguely, and almost admiringly.

"Weren't you afraid of traveling?"

"I was, for a week," she says. "I only lived on oranges for that time; I'd bought a bag of them the first day. That place creeped me out so bad, I couldn't get anything else down."

Even though she seems strong, I suddenly feel sorry for her. I have the feeling that I lay eyes on a different, vulnerable person behind the impression of superiority and strength she gives me.

"Why didn't you speak up?" I ask, leaning forward over the table. "It must have been uncomfortable."

She makes a face.

"Because I didn't want to admit that I'd done something stupid. It was, after all, better to stay. Besides, my parents had warned me against taking off. Only when I started getting so crazy with hunger that I almost couldn't get up out of bed, did I decide to return."

The wine bottle is just about empty, I'm feeling a bit drunk and strangely happy. It feels as if I'm falling in love. I wonder whether I should be honest and tell her about my experience. But I don't dare even though I ought to do it. I'm looking around in the bare room. From one of the other rooms, I can hear music and the sound of voices.

"The only thing I can do," she says, "is to wait for time to pass. In time, a way out may show up. There's nothing but to sit and wait."

Soon after, I reluctantly get up. It suddenly dawns on me that I've completely forgotten about the ad. That means I'll have to come back tomorrow.

"The last bus is leaving soon. I'll have to take off for home."

Helene looks at her watch. "Do you realize how late it is? You can sleep here if you want to."

I'm not sure I heard correctly, and I'm looking at her in surprise. "Yes, but…"

"There's no debate. It's so nice to wake up knowing I'm not alone."

I'm beginning to tingle a bit with excitement and anticipation. I hadn't imagined that. I decide to stay. I have to take the chance. I need to start living in the moment and forget everything I feel I have to do. There's nobody but myself I'm answerable to, and the moment may not come again.

"I've got to call home," I say.

She laughs.

I walk downstairs and call from the phone booth on the corner, but Mom and Dad must have gone to bed because they don't pick up the phone. I've never stayed away without telling where I am, and I have a bad conscience, but I try not to think of it. At the same time, I'm relieved that they don't know why I haven't come home. While I'm walking back up the stairs, my legs start shaking under me with excitement and anxiety.

When I step into the room, Helene is putting a sheet on a mattress that's lying on the floor.

"Is that where I'm supposed to sleep?" I exclaim in surprise.

"Yes."

I say nothing, but the last trace of my tipsiness disappears so suddenly that there's a ringing in my ears. I'm telling myself how stupid I've been. How could I think that she was interested in me? We're taking our clothes off with our backs turned to each other, and when I turn around, she's already lying in her bed. She reaches out her hand and takes a cigarette from the pack on the table.

"Aren't you going to bed?" she asks and strikes a match.

"Sure," I say, stumbling, while, without knowing why I do it, I'm taking three steps toward her bed and sitting down on its edge.

She's laughing quietly deep down in her throat. I'm sitting up, and I notice that my blood is pounding in my temples. I slowly raise one of my hands and let one of my fingers trace the lines on her face.

"You're beautiful," I say.

"I want to sleep now," she says and sits up, stubbing out her cigarette in the ashtray.

I hesitantly put my hands on the edge of the bed and am about to get up. Then a feeling that's stronger than my anxiety makes me let go, and I'm lowering my head down over hers. Her eyes are looking up into mine and her pupils are widening out of fear. She's pressing one hand against my chest, and I'm about to raise my head in disappointment, but then I notice that her lips are giving in.

* * *

My arm is falling asleep, but I don't move it because Helene's head is resting on it. I'm lying relaxed, listening to the deep, regular sounds of her breathing. The very fact that another person is lying by my side gets me to feel calmer, and it doesn't bother me that the light isn't on. I'm still amazed that I can experience the feelings she has made me feel.

I cautiously move my arm a little while I'm wondering if it's too noisy here for me to sleep, but fortunately there are no longer voices or music coming from the other rooms.

Suddenly, I hear that the locked door opens with a low click. I cautiously raise my head without moving my arm and see that a black figure is stepping into the dark light. Before I manage to react, the shadow stands behind my head and grabs my shoulders. A stream of little pricks is running down through my body, and a shock comes up from my belly. The two currents crash so violently into each other that my entire body comes into motion. With my teeth chattering, I'm beginning to rise from the bed until I support myself only with the back of my neck, my heels and the arm Helene's head lies on. My head is tilted over backward, my neck is stretched, and the rest of my body is extended in an arc, and a scream from halfway down is pushing up through my throat. I scream in horror, and I can't stop until the sound beats back against my ears. With jerky movements, I fall back down on the bed and gradually gain back control over my body.

I'm lying quite motionless, waiting for the light to come on. I must have screamed almost directly into Helene's ear, and I can imagine how the other residents are stirring outside the door because they think a crime has happened. With my inner eye, I can see what the headlines are going to look like if what I imagine they're thinking is true: Young Girl Murdered by Madman. What will Helene come to think of me? When the light is switched on, will I have to admit that I'm insane? Then it occurs to me that there's another option. I can explain that I suffer from nightmares. The thought helps me gradually settle down, and I'm beginning to wait almost impatiently for the reaction to my scream. I hadn't figured that the devil would return.

Nothing happens, and that surprises me. Helene is drawing her breath deeply and regularly, and I can't hear any sound from the hallway. My thoughts are impossible to control. Only a deaf person would have been able to sleep through my scream. Does it mean that I didn't scream? Does it also mean that I didn't rise up from the bed in an arc? I wonder if I should get out before she wakes up. I could leave a message saying that I had to take off because Mom and Dad don't know where I'm at. I'm lying motionless while the skeletons in my unconscious are sticking their bones into my eyes.

Helene wakes me up by shaking my arm. She stands leaning over and smiles at me, and I tentatively smile back. Last night's experience is still present in me, and the only thing I can think of is that I should have left. I don't know what to do, and I'm trying to discern a reaction on her part. Although I'm telling myself that it's impossible, I'm afraid that she heard my scream.

We're having breakfast, accompanied by clinking knives. Perhaps it's my nervousness that transmits itself to her, for every time one of us says something the other winces. Our voices sound much too loud in the quiet.

I'm feeling almost pathologically self-conscious. I can see us from outside or from a distance like a scene in a theater play. Here is sitting the crazy boy, and here is sitting the normal girl, and they're eating breakfast after they've spent the night in her bed. I should have told her about my experience, and, at the same time, I'm relieved I didn't. She may not have wanted to see me again.

I'm trying to drag out time because I can't get myself to leave. That makes me think of Mom and Dad who're waiting for me and don't know where I am.

Finally, I'm getting up reluctantly.

Helene puts down her knife and looks up. "What are you going to do today?" she asks.

"That ad I told you about," I say. "I've thought of going out there and looking at things more closely before I go home."

I'm getting up, taking my coat and buttoning it up, but I still can't make myself leave. I think that I can sense a tense silence on her part, but I'm not sure. I hesitantly start walking toward the door. Then I turn. I have to get over myself. It feels as though the blood is pressing into my face.

"Will we see each other again?" I ask and think that anyone else would have gone ahead and kissed her.

"Yes," she says and smiles.

I start laughing with relief.

"What are you laughing at?" she asks.

"Nothing," I say.

"When will we meet again?" she asks.

When we've promised each other to meet in three days, I walk down to the phone booth to call and tell where I've been.

The woman behind the counter looks like Mom. She is taking out a form.

After having left Helene's and having talked with Dad on the phone, I'm feeling happy, almost exuberant, and I think that I'm falling in love. That's why I've had this sudden impulse. At the same time, I'm glad to be alone. Since yesterday so much has happened that I need to think through by myself.

"Do you know what grade point average is required?" the woman asks and hands me the schedule and a folder.

"Yes."

"Do you have other educational assets or experiences from a stay abroad or anything else that can give you points?"

"No," I say.

I'm rolling up the application form and the folder about studying Danish and leave the office. The way seemingly trivial things can assume meaning puzzles me. So could my high school certificate be of use after all, and it will certainly help that I've read so much.

I take the first bus that leaves from the university, and while we're driving, I take the ad out of my pocket and read it. I'm sorry Susanne isn't with me, and I'm beginning to get nervous about what Mom and Dad will say. Perhaps I'm taking a poorly thought-out step.

The door is locked with a safety chain, and the man who snaps it open looks different than I had imagined. He's overweight and wearing a black set of clothes, greasy and with dandruff on the shoulders, and on the lapel of his jacket, there are dried traces of food. For some reason, I get the impression of something elegant that's gone to pot. Dry heat and a smell of mothballs come out of the door. The man kicks back a gray poodle that's coming out.

I'm losing courage.

"Yes," he says. "The room is still for rent. Are you sure you want it?"

"I'd like to see it first," I say uncertainly.

He sighs.

"One moment," he says and closes the door.

When he has removed the safety chain, he comes out into the hallway in slippers.

He's puffing and groaning while we're climbing up the stairs, and he takes a break at each floor. I almost have a bad conscience, making him walk all the way up to the fifth floor, but I want to see the room before I rent it.

There's a long hallway with a cocoanut-runner and a row of doors painted green, and the walls are covered in faded wallpaper with flowers on it. Out of breath, he opens the second door and steps aside while he is drying the sweat off his forehead with a handkerchief.

"It's this room that's for rent," he says.

I'm looking in. There's an old blue square felt rug on the floor with burn marks from cigarettes. The walls are white with yellow and brown stains as if someone had spilled coffee or beer on them. There's only one window in one side of the slanted wall, which gives the room a strangely one-eyed appearance as if it leaked out to one side. I'm glad Mom and Dad aren't with me. I'm sure that they wouldn't like it, that they'd be ashamed for me.

Through the walls, which look thin, I can hear sounds and voices from the surrounding rooms. I'm thinking how I can only fall asleep if it's completely still, and how I'm awakened by even the slightest noise. I don't know if I'll be able to sleep here, but I can't afford a more expensive room.

"Are you taking it?"

"Yes," I say.

"We only rent to decent people," he says and looks me up and down. "But you do look pretty decent."

When we're about to leave, a young guy is coming down the hallway. He sticks his head in.

"Good morning," he says to the landlord. "I want to make a complaint that the drain in the bathroom is stopped up again."

Then his gaze turns to me.

"Are you the new tenant?"

"Yes."

The landlord sighs.

"I'll look into it."

When the young guy is gone, he says, "Let's go down and sign the contract."

"I'll first have to talk to my parents," I say and become even more nervous about what they'll say. Maybe I haven't thought the matter through well enough. Maybe they'll forbid me to move.

"Then it's not for sure that the room will be available."

"I have to do that," I say.

Having seen the room, I have a feeling that it's not one that will rent out immediately.

We're walking down the stairs. Inside his apartment, there's heavy furniture everywhere, and the smell of mothballs is overpowering. The landlord's wife, who has a narrow face with a thin pointed nose, is sitting in a chair next to a heater under the window with a blanket over herself. The poodle is jumping up against me and going under cover underneath her chair while doing so. The husband asks for my address and phone number if he's supposed to hold the room, and in return I ask him to loan me the key so I can look at the room once more.

"Throw the key in through the mail slot when you come back," he says.

I walk up and let myself in. It's a depressing room, but I won't be able to afford a better one. And I'm convinced that it's important that I make myself independent of Mom and Dad. Again, I'm thinking about what they're going to say. Even though I'm beginning to function normally, I'm still not well. I don't know whether I'll manage to live on my own.

I walk out and look at the bathroom where long hairs are floating in the stopped-up sink. While I'm standing in the kitchen, the young guy comes out of his room.

I feel that I need to start a conversation to make a good impression. The only thing I can think of saying is, "Maybe you've also just moved in?"

He looks at me. Then he starts laughing. "No," he says.

* * *

"A room! You can't be serious," says Mom.

Though I tried to prepare myself during the bus ride, I get the sense that this is becoming more uncomfortable than I'd imagined.

"I didn't know that things were so bad. I didn't know that you hated me so much."

"I don't hate you."

"Sure you do," she says. "And Dad blames me for the fact that you got sick. It's because of me that you want to get away."

I look at Dad in surprise. That one I didn't hear before.

"I didn't say it was your fault," he says.

"No, but I can tell by your silence. You're trying to freeze me out."

Dad falls silent, but he has an angry and hurt expression in his face.

"It would be better if I moved out," she says. "Then you guys could be here alone. You've always gotten along better with each other. I never thought that I'd see this day. That you throw me out as your mother."

"Well, isn't it very natural that I'm moving out?" I say. "That's what all others my age do."

"But will you be able to make it?" asks Dad. "You know you're not well."

"I don't know," I say. "But I won't find out unless I try."

After all the years of quarreling and after my suicide attempt, I find it hard to understand why they're not relieved that I'm moving out. It may have been naive on my part, but in my insecurity, I'd hoped for their understanding and support.

"Aren't you guys glad that I'm getting an education?"

"We sure are," says Dad, "but we thought you'd keep studying while living at home. Think about how you can get messed up. You're far too naive. You know, you really don't know anything."

"I don't become less naive from not trying," I say.

"You're like me," says Mom. "You're afraid of other people."

"No," I say. "I'm not anymore. I think I'm growing strong."

"Where do you get such ideas from? Is it Susanne who's put that thought in your head?" she asks. "Or is it perhaps this girl you told us you met?"

"No."

"Don't you think you ought to stay home for a year." asks Dad. "Let's say nothing happens. By that time, you'll be doing better. You only just stopped taking pills."

"I need to move out," I say.

Mom raises her head and cradles it in her hands.

"I can remember when you'd just been born," she says. "It was so safe there when I was sitting with you on my lap. I wished so much I could stop time. I would wish that you hadn't grown older."

She turns her face to me. "I'm sure you won't even come and visit us. It's not just me, it's the whole place that you can't stand, right?"

I hesitate. "Well, yes," I say, "I hate this place."

"Are you ashamed of us?" she asks.

"No."

"I don't believe that," she says and turns around to face Dad. "Can you understand that?" she says to him. "We're no longer good enough."

"I don't understand why you think things will be so very different if you move to another town," he says.

"It's not just a question of moving," I say. "It's a question of starting out on my own."

I'm trying not to show how terrified I am.

"You're not allowed to."

"I'm moving out," I say in a low voice.

"What kind of place is it?"

"It's a room I can afford to pay for," I say.

I'm glad they haven't seen it.

"So you're moving out," says Mom. "There's nothing more we can do?"

"No."

She gets up. "Don't come back and tell us we didn't warn you."

When she's gone, Dad gets up and stands by the window.

"It's going to be empty here without you," he says. He turns and looks out the window. "When you didn't come home last night…we didn't know whether we should call the police and have them start a search. We thought that…that…"

"I'm sorry," I say. "I do know that was very thoughtless of me, but you'd gone to bed."

"Do you know how old I am?" he asks. "I'll die soon. I thought I could rely on you until such a time. You know how afraid you mother is of illness."

He puts his hands on the desk. "Can you imagine how lonely she'll be when you've moved out and I'm no longer around?"

I can feel how the last shreds of my self-control are evaporating, and I'm beginning to shake.

"Dad, you mustn't push me to stay," I say. "Think about how it would be if I stayed only because I'm waiting for you to die. Mom and I would end up killing each other."

* * *

The driver has been waiting impatiently with the engine running.

"Will you call when you arrive?" says Dad. "There must be a phone booth nearby."

"Yes."

In the two days since I told them that I would be moving out, Mom has not wanted to talk to me. But I've firmly decided to move. I have a feeling that I'd perish if I kept living at home.

I'm shaking hands with Dad and we're standing stiffly, like strangers to each other. When I reach for Mom's hand, I realize to my dismay that she won't give it to me. She's looking away, and I have a sense that she's trying to control herself. Then she sticks out her hand, but without looking at me.

I climb up into the cabin with the driver. I still have a feeling that there's something I need to talk about with Mom and Dad, but I don't know what it could be. I place a suitcase with some of my books on my knees.

"Is that the last one?" asks the driver.

"Yes."

"Do you know the address?"

"Yes."

"Good. Let's go."

I'm waving out of the window. I'm feeling astounded and sad that even the farewell can soften Mom. Dad has his hand up and is waving back, and at the last moment, when the truck is about to turn around the corner, Mom suddenly raises her hand too and waves.

The driver turns on the car radio, and I'm settling into my seat. In the last days, everything has happened so fast. I'm afraid of the new, but not as afraid as I'd imagined I'd be. What I feel most strongly is a will to live, and I have a distressing sense of having wasted time. I don't know if I'll ever be normal.

I lift the lid of my suitcase and look down at the bottles with the last of my pills and the envelope with the prescription which I've hidden as a bit of insurance. All of a sudden, I'm seized by a powerful anxiety at the thought of how lonely it will be in the room. I will be alone, fearful of loneliness, fearful of taking the decisive step, fearful of the feeling of anxiety itself. For a moment, I consider asking the driver to turn around. I'm trying to monitor myself and to mobilize my defenses. I know two people, and after the summer, I'll probably get started on an education.

I notice that it gives me a sense of security that in the course of the last year, I've experienced the worst I can imagine. I don't think that much of anything I'm going to encounter going forward will be as distressful as what happened.

The thought helps me relax slowly, and I'm feeling calmer.

When I arrive, I'll put a match to the prescription and watch it burn in the ashtray. Then I'll go to the bathroom and flush the pills down the toilet. There mustn't be any way of return.

I'm leaning back in my seat.

Printed in Great Britain
by Amazon